JANET HOGGARTH

Gaby's Angel

OXFORD

UNIVERSITY PRESS

OXFORD
UNIVERSITY PRESS

Great Clarendon Street, Oxford OX2 6DP
Oxford University Press is a department of the University of Oxford.
It furthers the University's objective of excellence in research, scholarship,
and education by publishing worldwide in

Oxford   New York

Auckland   Cape Town   Dar es Salaam   Hong Kong   Karachi
Kuala Lumpur   Madrid   Melbourne   Mexico City   Nairobi
New Delhi   Shanghai   Taipei   Toronto

With offices in

Argentina   Austria   Brazil   Chile   Czech Republic   France   Greece
Guatemala   Hungary   Italy   Japan   Poland   Portugal   Singapore
South Korea   Switzerland   Thailand   Turkey   Ukraine   Vietnam

Oxford is a registered trade mark of Oxford University Press
in the UK and in certain other countries

British Library Cataloguing in Publication Data

Data available

ISBN: 978-0-19-274548-4

1 3 5 7 9 10 8 6 4 2

Printed in Great Britain
Paper used in the production of this book is a natural,
recyclable product made from wood grown in sustainable forests
The manufacturing process conforms to the environmental
regulations of the country of origin

This book is for my three little angels:

Lilla, Teya and Danny.

I wouldn't have got through it without you.

CONTENTS

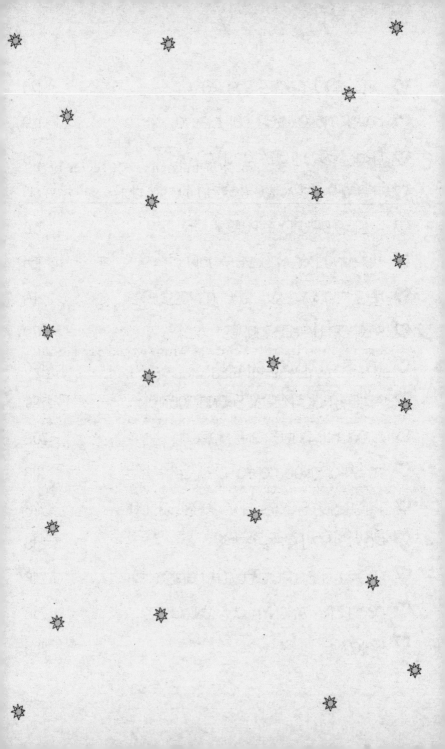

PROLOGUE

Have you ever thought you might have a secret best friend? One that no one else can see? *Really*, you have? Let me ask you this then—are you mad? Seriously, think about it, it *is* a bit crazy, isn't it? Having a best friend that only *you* can see. That only happens when you're four and bored with playing Barbies on your own and Ken just doesn't cut the mustard any more. But when you get to my age, (thirteen in case you are wondering), it just gets a bit too beardy-weirdy as Mum would say (about the man in the health-food shop. Yes, he has a beard and yes he is a bit weird and yes he talks about crystals and stuff). So if you ever find yourself in a tricky situation like me, with an actual virtual best friend, or to be more precise a dead best friend, don't call for the men in white coats. Because what you may be experiencing, dear reader, is not the total breakdown of your one-celled brain, but, in fact, your very own angel . . .

EmbaRRaSSiNg DiSCO AntiCS
SePtembeR

'No one is going to turn up,' I wailed to Emily who was leaning sideways on the range cooker in the kitchen filing her nails and looking at me like I was a specimen in a Petri dish. 'It's going to be the biggest flop since chocolate radiators.'

'What on earth are you talking about, you muppet. Of course people will turn up. It's Us. We have good parties!'

She was right; every party I can remember since I had a memory, so about aged three, we've had joint spectacular birthday parties. Admittedly, they were really for the grown-ups so that they could get drunk and cry about how their babies were growing up too fast and then all be in a hideous grump the next day complaining that the TV was too loud, or whatever. As the years went on, it was expected that we, Emily and I, would continue with the joint parties and that they would be a total laugh, for the kids and grown-ups alike. Dad used to be a DJ back in the day (now has a much more sober job in IT) and Mum is a fashion stylist, though she doesn't do it so much more now, she helps out in Marisa's shop (Marisa is Emily's mum who owns The Brown Bag, an über-cool clothes shop on the high street with a cappuccino machine in it for peeps browsing the racks). This year it was our turn to host the party and as luck would have it, the weather was a blazing Indian summer haze one week into the autumn term at school. Dad had set his decks up in the garden—he played things called vinyl! Now whoever heard of that? Old skool or what!!! iPod who? For someone who works in technology he has a funny way of keeping up with the times. 'Darling— an iPod is all very well, but real music is better when it crackles and jumps a bit and you have to actually put the needle on the record. It's a ritual.' He's a bit mad, my dad. Ritual? Just plug the iPod in and you're away.

'Aha, I've just got it,' Emily looked triumphantly at me and waved her emery board in my face nearly taking my eye out.

2

'Got what?'

'Why you're so bothered about the fact that no one will come.'

'Enlighten me,' I said twiddling with my gold heart-shaped pendant round my neck; Emily had a matching one. On one side it had our names engraved and on the back it said Friends Forever. We had given them to each other for this year's birthday. I loved them. So far, I had worn mine at every given opportunity (apart from at school; jewellery was banned).

'It's because Jake's going to be coming.' Whoosh, someone set my face on fire and now it was hot enough to BBQ on. Ouch! Step away from the flames, Gaby Richards.

'Nooooo! It's not because of that; I just think this year people might not come.' I wasn't even convincing myself.

'Whatever, you ain't kidding me, honey!' Emily drawled in a fake American accent. She always did the fake accent when she knew I was on a great cover up scheme. And, yes, I was a bit bothered because Jake was coming. But I didn't want to say it out loud; the minute you say stuff out loud, it's real and when it's real, that's when it can come back to haunt you. Deny, deny deny—that's my motto!

So . . . Jake. You want me to explain, huh? Okey-dokey—but he's just a *boy*. He's not really *that* important. Let's start with Emily first. Emily and I have been best friends since we were bumps at our mums' ante-natal classes. They used to go out and eat cake and then when we came along they ate even more cake (according to them to stop themselves from going mad looking after babies). Lucky for us we actually liked each other or it would have been one of those awkward friend-ships where you have to get on because your mums are friends. Those type of friends *suck*! Mum tried to make me like her friend Lucy's little girl, Emma, but Emma always used to poke me in the eye when Mum wasn't looking and spit in my juice or snatch toys. Oh, and her favourite ploy was to smile and say she liked me when I left and would I come again—all the while pulling faces at me as I walked out of the door. Mum and Lucy don't see each other any more and I'd be surprised if Emma has any friends at all!

Anyway, blabing on again (Emily says I could talk at the Olympics and win Gold, Silver, and Bronze as no one would come near to beating me). You think? Gosh so, yeah, Em and I are BFFs (Best Friends Forever if you are clueless and live in a cave). Emily is your basic nightmare as a best friend. She is the Pretty One. I am the . . . now, what am I? The Chatty One with the Big Ears? Yes, but that makes me sound like I would have to be Shrek and to make up for it I have a motor mouth. The Funny One with the Big Ears? I can tell a few jokes, but to be honest, humour is not my forte. I am the One With the Glass Eye, and the Big Ears. That one is a lie of course. I am the . . . the . . . er . . . Quirky One. Yes, I like that. And as you may have guessed, I have a bit of a phobia about my ears.

So, triple medal winner in blahing on and still no nearer to knowing who Jake is. With Emily being Emily, the Pretty One, I don't stand any chance of bagging a second look from most boys in our class. Or do I? And really, are there any worth getting a second look from? Most boys are, in my humble opinion, wooden like Pinocchio. So dull dull dull. And Real Boys only exist in the years above or on the telly.

After the summer hols some of the boys had their strings cut, according to Emily, i.e. turned into Real Boys. And one of those previous Pinocchios had been Jake. It's amazing what a bit of sunshine, ten centimetres, and a trendy haircut can do for a puppet. Why, Jake, you are a Real Boy! And that's when it hit me, that maybe I liked him. Noooooo! I prided myself on *never* liking anyone that might be vaguely attainable. So pop stars, older boys, and even (don't repeat this) someone from a children's TV programme when I was younger!

And after noticing Jake was a Real Boy, Emily saw that I couldn't even look at him and invited him and Robbie (his best friend and total admirer of Emily) to our birthday party without even asking me. We usually only have girls. 'It's about time we branched out, Gabs. We've been at Heathside a year now, it's not baby school. Boys are part of our lives whether you like it or not.' Why???????? I liked it when it was all Pinocchios and liking people you couldn't have. Why did we have to go up a gear? The two boys asked if they could bring friends, so of course I said no and Em said yes. 'They need to have friends, Gabs. Boys are like dogs—they travel in packs and if they feel out of their comfort zone, they're boring. They need playmates, or we'll have to babysit them and I'm not doing that at our party.' Fair point, I suppose.

'Next you'll be saying you invited Alexandra Bennett!'

'Oh dear, I have, would that be so terrible?'

'Argh! You're impossible, I can't bear her, she'll walk round the house with her coolometer measuring how trendy my house is and then only manage to give a compliment about anything when it's really meant as an insult, and then walk off smiling like she's queen bee. Noooooooo!'

Emily was laughing now. 'Of course I haven't invited her, you muppet, she's a total cow. Calm down and put your eyes back in—they're all bulgy and mad!'

As you guessed, Alexandra Bennett drives me mad. I can't bear insults in disguise—it's so confusing! If you want to be horrible, just be horrible, don't pretend to be nice and then stick the knife in. She is the year trendsetter and possessor of all-round knowledge on what's hot and what's not, her and her pack of mates (Kool Aids as we call them). Handy with free-flying fake niceness. Yuck!

So, here we are and no one has turned up and I am pacing the floor while Mum and Marisa knock back the wine and empty nachos into stylish ceramic bowls and scrape posh dips into ramekins so it all looks just so. That's the trouble with having mums who are into fashion; every event is like a magazine shoot!

Fast forward to an hour later and the house is heaving, the russet autumn garden is getting trampled by everyone and Dad is on the decks doing embarrassing hands-in-the air moves to some old tunes only the grown-ups know. 'Dad, can you ditch the rave music—can we have Abba?' so he digs around and produces it. All the girls from school hit the floor (or should I say chewed-up lawn) while the boys lurk on the patio trying not to stare at Emily and failing, cos she looks so cool in her little baby-blue jumpsuit showing off her tanned legs and tossing her mane of golden hair. If she wasn't my best friend I would hate her!

It was weird having boys at the party—I wasn't sure I liked it. And I disliked it even more when something very unGaby-like happened. Dad changed the tune to some dodgy old disco track, and Emily dragged Robbie up from the side of the garden where he was catching flies with his open gob looking at her, and so the first boy was on the dance floor. Robbie kept signalling like a madman to Jake with his head, jerking to the side—it was about to fall off. Jake went so red I thought his ears might start to smoke. I turned to Rosie, one of our other friends, and was about to see if she wanted to come up and dance, but she was stuffing a rather large piece of quiche into her mouth, so I turned back and Jake was standing right in front of me zapping my personal space. I jumped back and knocked into one of the mums, who spilt red wine all down her white hippie blouse thing and bashed rice salad into my hair. Brilliant. 'Sorry, really sorry,' I whimpered. She looked like she wanted to punch me one in the face, but because it was my party and I was a child, she couldn't!

'That's fine, it was an accident.' Yeah, right and you will be kicking a stone in a second pretending it's my head.

I had wine in my hair stuck to oily grains of brown rice and slimy red onion. A piece of feta cheese slid down my cheek. 'Do you want to dance?' Jake stammered. It was dripping down my neck. Hang on—what did he say?

'What?' I barked.

'Do you want to dance?' Some of the mums were nudging each other and pulling 'Bless him' faces. Oh, the shame.

'No, I've got wine and cheese in my hair.' Nice, good come-back, except you do want to dance with him.

Rosie heard him. 'I'll come. Wait a sec while I finish my quiche,' and she charmingly wolfed down the last bit and grabbed Jake's hand and dragged him into the midst of gyrating girls. How to dazzle a boy into liking you, telling him you have a cheese and wine cocktail in your hair while turning him down at a disco. Gaby, you know all the tricks . . .

THE DREADED ACCIDENT

'I never knew Rosie fancied Jake,' George whispered to Em and me on the bus on Monday. Rosie was a few rows in front and daydreaming with her iPod plugged in.

'She doesn't,' Emily said.

'But she spent the rest of the party dancing with him. She didn't even have more food—very unlike her.' Rosie liked her food. It came before most things. But annoyingly she wasn't fat.

'I think Jake likes Gaby,' Em announced to our crowd. Our crowd being me, Em, Rosie (but she was plugged in), George, and Millie.

'Emily—he does not!' I shouted, so loudly that in fact Rosie looked up and so did half the bus, including

Robbie at the front. I didn't know where Jake was. Thank heavens above he wasn't on the bus.

'I think he does too,' George piped up.

'He wants to marry you, he wants to kiss you, he wants to love you, he wants to marry you, ooh ooh ooh ooooooooooh ooh . . .' sang Millie swinging her shoulders and wagging her finger in the style of Beyoncé like she was on the *X Factor*.

'Yeah, hey, funny. F. U. N. N. Y.,' I spelt out. He did not. But what if he did? What happens when they *do* like you? What do you do?

'Whatever—he fancies you, accept it!' Emily looked triumphant. 'Oh, look we're here.'

The bus stopped right outside the school gates on the main road. Emily jumped up as she was next to the aisle and got pushed along in the melee. 'I'll see you out there!' she shouted over her shoulder and winked at me, our secret wink. I struggled with my massive maxi purple patent-leather bag (it could have housed a family of five, maybe it did, I couldn't lift it!). By the time I had wrestled it out from under the seat the bus was half empty and all the girls had got off. I raced to the front and jumped down into the sunshine, my new school shoes making a satisfying clunk on the pavement. This Indian summer just kept on giving. Em was waiting to cross the road with the girls, but she wasn't looking as her phone started ringing so she rooted in her bag. One of the girls stepped in the road but stepped back because they saw the car coming.

It is a cliché, but what happened next all happened in slow motion. I couldn't get to her to stop her stepping out—there were too many kids in the way. Nothing would come out of my mouth, it was like one of those dreams when you know you have to scream but you can't make a sound. George looked up just as Emily stepped off the kerb and tried to grab her bag strap and missed, so she shouted her name and Emily turned her head, but it was too late, the car hit her.

George got to her first. I remember one of the sixth form lads screaming, 'Don't move her, leave her head alone,' and he pushed everyone out of the way. Cars were stopping and causing a roadblock, kids were screaming. I just stared while the sixth form boy listened to her chest. By now teachers were running out onto the road. Mr Philips, head of PE, shouted: 'Has anyone called an ambulance?' as he knelt down beside Emily and talked to the sixth form boy, who shook his head. Mr Philips listened to her chest and started CPR. I couldn't watch. George was cradling my head and Robbie was next to me, holding my hand. In any other scenario, having Robbie holding my hand would have been the biggest story of the day, but right now, I think he needed to do it. 'Don't die, Em, don't die,' I could hear someone sobbing. 'Please God, let her live. Don't die.' Tears were running down my face and I was shaking. The voice was coming from me. From behind the self-made roadblock of cars I could hear sirens. Cars started to move and crawl past the scene and suddenly two ambulances and two police cars arrived and a flurry of activity exploded with paramedics jumping this way and that and police putting up cones and directing traffic. Em was still flat out on the road but I couldn't see what was happening as there were so many paramedics and police, we all had to take quite a few steps back. The teachers were shepherding people back into school. They came to try and move Robbie, George, me, Rosie, and Millie. 'No, I'm not going in,' I said in a low voice.

'Come on, leave the paramedics to do their job,' Mrs Thornton, our English teacher coaxed softly.

'I'm not leaving her,' I wailed. My legs gave way and I collapsed on the floor and after that I don't remember much of anything else . . .

Emily died, straight away, so they think. She hit her head on the edge of the kerb and that was what did it. I have a hazy memory of lying down in the sick room with George holding my hand and Rosie and Millie stroking my hair. All three of them sobbing. I was sick into the waste-paper bin—that I do remember. It had holes in and it went all over the carpet. Apparently school closed that day. Kids were milling around waiting for parents to pick them up. Mum came and got me and took the girls home too until their mums could come and get them. Mum was white as a sheet when she picked us up. I couldn't stop crying when I saw her and neither could she.

I couldn't look at the place where Emily had lain when we passed it in the car. I closed my eyes and when I did I saw her winking at me, like she had just before she got off the bus. *Oh, Em, I didn't get to you in time. I should have got to you. I let you down.*

The main criminal in all of this sat looking at me from my lap. My purple maxi bag. Right then, on the hideous journey home, I hated that bag more than anything in the whole world. If that flipping bag hadn't got stuck under the seat because it was just *too big*, I would have been standing next to Em and none of this would have happened. We would be in Maths now, cheating in our test and giggling.

We pulled up outside our house and as soon as we got inside, I emptied my bag all over the floor. 'What are you doing?' Mum asked while the girls watched me, looking worried. I had obviously flipped or something.

'Chucking this stupid bag in the bin,' I shouted and opened the front door and ran to the green wheelie bin at the front gate, lifted the lid and hurled the culprit right in there. When I came back in the house Mum was picking up all my stuff off the floor. She didn't say a word. I actually didn't want to be there, with anyone, the girls, Mum, anyone. I didn't say a word either, I just took myself up to my room and shut the door behind me and the first thing I saw was a picture of Emily pinned to the corner of my dressing table mirror. I ripped it off and held it really tight, willing her to be OK, knowing she was dead but not quite believing it. I lay on my bed, the bed we used to bounce on and pretend it was a trampoline until Mum banged on the ceiling and shouted up the stairs. Hot stinging tears pricked my eyes and just kept on spilling silently down my face, filling my ears, soaking my neck, blurring everything. 'So this is what a broken heart feels like,' I wailed out loud.

'Oh, Gaby,' Mum cried—she must have been hovering outside. She took me in her arms like she did when I was still her baby and cradled me. I thought I was going to be sick with pain in my chest. 'Just let it all out.'

But there really was nothing to let out. After that initial sob fest, nothing. No words were formed or said out loud. I had stopped crying and just lay there staring, eyes blinking because they were now so dry.

'I know this is a stupid question, but do you want to eat anything? You haven't eaten since breakfast and the girls said you were sick in the bin.' Eat? Was she mad? I couldn't eat if you paid me.

'Maltesers,' I squeaked. 'Can I have some Maltesers?' Who said that? Did I say it? I *hate* Maltesers. They taste of Horlicks and that is so like a crime. Emily always loved Maltesers, in fact our birthday cake this year was covered half in Maltesers for her and half in mini Dime bars for me. Yes, Dime bars, the most underestimated choc bar there is. The chocolate was just so creamy and the brittle toffee centre had just the right amount of caramel flavour and minuscule touch of saltiness to stop it being super sickly. Thus allowing you to eat at least three . . . So why was I craving Maltesers?

Mum looked at me oddly and nodded. 'I'll just go to the shop. Do you want one of the girls up here with you?' I shook my head. All I wanted was to be on my own now.

I don't know how long I lay there. I drifted off to sleep; well I must have. The next thing I knew we were at school and just getting off the bus and I was next to Emily and she was looking in her bag to get her ringing phone and the car was coming, but I was next to her and I grabbed her as she stepped out without looking and the red car zoomed past, ruffling our skirts. 'That was close,' she said. 'I think you just saved my life.' And she laughed and looked at her phone to see who had called. And then I woke up and the Maltesers were on my chest as I lay on my bed. Even though I felt sick, sick, sick, for some reason I felt compelled to eat them. So I pulled myself up and had started to open the packet when Mum walked in with another packet of them in her hand.

'Oh, where d'you get those from?' she asked all surprised. 'I just went to get you some.'

'But I thought you already had,' I said, feeling a bit confused.

'No, I just got back.' We both looked at each other like we were a bit bonkers.

'Maybe one of the girls sneaked them up while I was asleep,' I suggested.

'Maybe . . .' She trailed off, not sounding convinced. 'Oh well, you can have two packets now.'

She put them on the bed next to me and left quietly. I bit into my first Malteser for years. It was *amazing*. How had I ever thought they were minging? Emily was right; they really were little balls of delight. And thinking of her made me stop and I put the packet down and wondered again about how I got that bag of Maltesers on my chest. I would ask the girls, but you know, really it just wasn't important. Nothing was any more. Oh, Em, what was I going to do without you . . . ?

BaCK to tHe ReaL WORLD

The funeral was a total nightmare. Not because anything
bad happened, just because it was a funeral and I had
never been to one before. The church was bursting at
the seams. Marisa—Dave—Em's dad, and her younger
brother, Gus, were at the front and we were a few rows
behind them. Max, my younger brother, was there too.
No one was wearing black—Marisa had asked them
not to. I was wearing my gorgeous purple silky Topshop tea dress I had worn at our birthday party a few
weeks before. Even Alexandra Bennett was there. Why
was she there? I couldn't stand her. But then everyone
across all the cliques loved Emily. I was half expecting
her to make a comment on how a white coffin would be

so last year, and then hadn't the energy to finish off my internal bitching session.

The days after the accident all merged into one. Each was the same, punctuated only by the same waking thought: maybe it was all just a bad dream. Every day I blamed myself. I know George was going down that road too. She couldn't forgive herself for not trying harder to grab the bag strap. Poor Mum didn't know what to do with me. I couldn't eat, sleep or even watch TV. I know when I can't watch TV it's an emergency. Worst of all, the delicious Belgian waffles that Mum hates me eating were going mouldy in the bread bin. Not even all their preservatives could save them now.

Sitting in the ancient ornate church waiting for the shuffling to stop and people to settle, I looked around. Not being a church regular I was transfixed by all the stained-glass windows. I must have daydreamed because one of the windows had a scene with an angel blowing a horn and another angel laughing. The angel laughing looked just like Emily. I looked again and the angel winked at me. I jumped. 'Are you OK, darling?' Mum said in a soothing voice, her hand shaking as she patted my arm. I looked at her to see if she had seen it too. No, just me. Lack of sleep, obviously. I did feel dizzy and sick and suddenly had a mad craving for Maltesers again. I hadn't eaten them since the day Emily . . . *died*. I can't even say the word yet without wanting to cry.

Just then music started playing and everyone stood up. It was Emily's favourite tune. A song called 'Run'. I thought I might pass out from restraining the urge to . . . run from the church and away from it all and just not face the fact that we were standing here, in this church, to say goodbye to my best friend: the sister I wished was mine, the girl everyone wanted to be friends with or wanted to be like, the kindest, funniest, smartest, most beautiful girl I have ever known. How could this be happening? Things like this happen on the telly, not in real life. Why? Why? Why? Why? The slender white coffin topped with wobbling delicate pink flowers and a rose love-heart passed by carried by the undertakers, the only people wearing black on this cloudy September morning. Mum was weeping gripping my hand and holding Max's hand in the other. Dad was bawling his eyes out—I don't think I had ever seen him cry, apart from when Chelsea lost in some final or other and he had had too many beers. Max had his head buried in Mum's chest. Me, I was almost puking. I had to get out of there. I just didn't think I could handle it. I was next to the aisle, so I decided that as soon as the coffin was on the stand by the altar, I was outta there. And as the undertakers gently went down on their knees and skilfully manoeuvred the precious cargo into its resting place, I took my hand out of Mum's and started to move away. But Mum grabbed my hand even tighter and pulled me back. She whispered in my ear, 'You're not going anywhere, Yabba Gabba.' I looked to my right but Mum was rooting around in her bag on the floor to get tissues and handing them to Dad and Max. She turned to me, 'Would you like one, Gaby?' How could she have spoken to me and grabbed my hand when she was reaching in her bag right down there? And she never called me Yabba Gabba—that was my school nickname. I think I was having a funny turn, again. They happened so regularly now that it was almost unusual if I didn't feel a bit mental or bonkers.

We sat down and the rest of the service stretched out in front of me like a slow form of torture. But somehow, I felt much calmer and was able to listen to Emily's list of accomplishments and the poem that her dad had chosen to read. Her friends were spoken about—I got a special mention and Mum squeezed my hand at that part. Then it was time to go—the school choir sang us out with Robbie Williams's, 'Angels', and because they were a bit ropy, it took the edge off the procession out

22

of the church and I managed to smile. Emily would have been rolling her eyes at the bum notes they hit. There was a thing called a wake afterwards; the family were going to the crematorium now and we would meet back at their house and wait for them.

The sun came out and we drove back to our part of town, looking at people through the windows who didn't have to say goodbye to their best friend, who could enjoy the last few rays of the dying summer in the knowledge that tomorrow they would get up for school and moan about the test they had, or that it was raining and it was hockey. Small stuff. Stuff that I just didn't care about any more because what was the point? I just wanted to sleep, there and then in the car, and not wake up until I was really old, like twenty-five and completely sorted with a job, house, lots of cash and a mended broken heart. It must be so much easier being a grown-up.

I hadn't been at school for two weeks. As I said, those two weeks passed in a complete blur of uneaten plates of food and sleepless nights. I looked like a creature from the zombie movie: *The Night of the Living Dead*. Mum went to work—she had to, someone had to run Marisa's shop for her while she had a nervous breakdown. I didn't even see Marisa, Dave, or Gus before the funeral. What would I say? How would it be? Mum said she was beside herself, as you would be. Mum had obviously seen her and had been round there most days after the end of work to keep her posted on progress in The Brown Bag. I'm sure Marisa wouldn't care if The Brown Bag was abducted by aliens and set up shop on Mars.

I sat at the breakfast table, Mum and Dad pretending they weren't watching me like hawks, Max scoffing his Marmite toast, and Dog the cat winding itself round my chair leg wanting a stroke, so I idly scratched the top of her head sending her into spasms of delight. My Belgian waffle looked like it would rather be taken hostage by Max and cruelly torn up and eaten than sit abandoned on my plate, looking all forlorn and cardboard-like. It wasn't selling itself to me.

'Gaby, you have to eat.' Mum stated the obvious. I knew I had to eat. I only ate when it seemed I might pass out from exhaustion. My clothes didn't fit and I looked minging. My new school uniform felt like it was made for someone who had eaten all the pies, flapping round my tummy. I had to have a belt on the first notch to keep my skirt up. I didn't want to look like this. When I saw the girls at the funeral, they looked pretty beaten up, especially George, who wasn't fat, but was bigger

than me, she was now almost supermodel waif-like.
I hadn't seen them since the day they were here when
Emily . . . They kept ringing my phone and calling at
the house, but I couldn't face them. I only wanted Emily
and I couldn't have her, so I didn't want anyone else.

The waffle just wasn't doing it for me. My tummy
was in knots and my head felt like there was a houseful
of people living in there, all banging away with pots and
pans and opinions on how I should feel or not feel. 'Do
you want some toast instead?' I nodded, just to make
Mum feel happy. She spirited away the offending waffle
to the bin. Warm buttery white toast arrived in front
of me, raspberry jam on one piece and crunchy peanut
butter on the other so I could make my own sandwich,
a habit formed when I was a toddler, apparently. I dutifully did the honours and bit into it just to please Mum,
but it was actually quite comforting, so I managed to
eat it all.

'Come on, Gabs, get yer coat, we're off,' Dad said
in his fake Northern accent. He was from Yorkshire,
but had lost his accent years ago. But puts it on most
days, when he needs to be noticed. Dad was taking me
in to school so I didn't have to brave the bus on my
own, just for today. I had to finally take off my sacred
birthday pendant which so far had remained constantly

around my neck after Em . . . I felt like I was leaving her behind doing that but I didn't want it confiscated at school. Because I had thrown my school bag in the bin, Mum had bought me a new one from Topshop—silver leather, not a maxi bag but a slouchy bag with tassles on it. In my previous life I would have been screaming in delight; I could barely raise a smile when she gave it to me to fill up with all my bits and bobs. I slung it over my shoulder, the toast nearly making a guest re-appearance as I thought of passing the place in the car where Emily had . . .

Why did I have to go back to school? No one would miss me. I could live in my room till I was twenty-five and watch TV; I'm sure I would learn a lot more than in the classroom. I mean, who needs to know about physics unless you're going to be a scientist? I was going to be a . . . hmm, not quite sure what, but not a scientist. TV critic? I did have lots of experience . . . 'I hope it's OK,' Mum said as she hugged me close, kissing the top of my head. Max gave me a hug too. Even the cat was looking like she was moving in for a hug; oh no, that's right, Dog doesn't do affection, so she scratched my leg—her way of showing she cared. She drew blood. Nice.

I closed my eyes as we passed the dreaded black spot and pulled into the car park. Dad got out and opened

the door like a chauffeur. 'Chin up, duck. Deep breath.'
And he bear-hugged me till I thought all the breath had
escaped my lungs. He is a big man, Dad. 'Make sure you
eat your lunch—you're all skin and bone.' He got back
in the car and drove off. I watched till he pulled out of
the car park and turned towards the path up to the playground. I saw someone waving out of the corner of
my right eye, over by the art block. I turned and looked.
'Emily . . . ?' It was her, waving at me. I ran like a madwoman, pushing kids out of the way in my haste to get
to her. It was only a ten-second sprint, but when I got
to the place she had been, there was no one there. 'Em?
Where are you?' There was nowhere for her to have
gone. I twisted my head like an owl looking everywhere.
Then I looked down at my feet and there on the floor
was a perfectly white long elegant feather; I picked it up
and smelt it. Do not ask me why—it smelt of chocolate.
Now I knew I was bonkers. I put it in my new bag and
headed for the playground. What else could I do? This
was going to be one long day . . .

AN ARGUMENT AND AN UNEXPECTED VISITOR

'How you been, Yabba Gabba?' Rosie asked as I walked into the playground just before the bell. She looked tired, we all did. I was still reeling from my feather incident. This was the first time I had seen them since the funeral. And we didn't really chat much at the wake, no one did. It was lots of people pretending to drink tea and picking at the fairy cakes and sandwiches. It should have been called a sleep; it was so quiet.

'OK. You know, not great.'

'You look a bit thin, Gabs. Have you stopped eating the waffles?' George questioned. She wasn't looking so healthy herself.

'Yep, can't face them.' I didn't know what to say. What *do* you say? My life has been ripped apart and I can't be bothered with school, TV, magazines, talking, parents, going out, staying in, living, breathing, blah blah . . . Millie mooched over to me and just gave me a big hug, then Rosie did, followed by George, and we just stood there in the playground, hugging. I felt dead inside, but the hug felt good.

'It will be OK,' Millie whispered. 'We won't ever forget her, I promise.' I know why she was saying it: Emily was my best friend in the whole world, yes she was in our group, and yes she was bessie mates with all of us, but it was me and her together for ever, and everyone else knew that. I felt lost because the other three were each other's best friends. I had them too, but it wasn't the same, they were their own little group and that's how the dynamic of our friendship group had always worked.

'Thank you,' I stammered, grateful to have such brilliant friends. The bell rang and we unglued ourselves and headed down the steps into school for a scintillating day of learning and bettering ourselves. Just grrrrrrreat!

'So, how was the first week back?' Mum asked on Friday after she got in from The Brown Bag, clasping a bottle of wine and our fish and chips takeaway dinner (Friday treat). She started unwrapping the dinner from the grease-stained white paper and vinegary wafts of hot chip air filtered up my nostrils, making my mouth water—for the first time in ages. Max was hovering behind her as she plonked food on plates and he tried to steal chips while she batted his fingers away, nabbing a few for herself in the process.

I shrugged. School was school. I could describe how I had been treated like a cancer victim, was let off having to do tests, was allowed to stare aimlessly out of windows instead of actually participating in any learning and worst of all, was given a hug by our tutor group teacher, Miss Paxton (do you know about deodorant, Miss P?). Talking was boring, so I got by with shrugging and grimacing. I just could not be *bothered*! Even Alexandra Bennett, the class not-quite bully, hadn't said one snide remark. I was expecting some comment about my falling down skirt, but she bit her lip. It must have been excruciating for her to have to rein herself in.

'Aha, like that was it?' Mum said giving me a sideways glance. 'You'll have to talk at some point, Gaby.' I nodded. But not right now. I had managed a whole week of doing my clam impression and just speaking when I had to. Right now I was going to eat the first meal in

a few weeks that tickled my fancy. So, I guess for the pur-
poses of my very super-duper interesting story, we will
have to hit the fast-forward button or you guys will be
asleep. The next few weeks went something like this:
sleepovers: invited to three—attended—none; cinema
trips: invited to ten—attended—none; after-school roll-
erblading: invited constantly—attended—none; me feeling like I wanted to smash things at the unfairness of it all:
a million times—threw a teddy at my bedroom wall; sight-
ings of Emily at school and in the street: so many it was
freaky—I was obviously *mental*; cravings for Maltesers: a
million—a million packets consumed, who knew?; wanting to sit in my room and be on my own: all the time—
yep, you guessed it, so that's what I did. I wanted to snap
out of it, I really did, but it was almost comforting not to
try any more and just exist. I knew what everyone thought
and I knew the girls were losing patience with me, but it
was almost impossible now to turn it around and start
doing stuff. Mum and Dad were whispering about coun-
selling and every time they did, I shouted at them to leave
me alone. As for Jake, I had forgotten all about him . . .

It was George's birthday and the last day before half
term, and she always had a Hallowe'en party as her

31

birthday is October 31st. I watched as the girls got excited about it over lunch. I had an invite, but obviously had not replied. I wasn't going to go—why change the habit of my new lifetime.

'I think Robbie's going to come, and Jake,' Rosie said excitedly. 'We can play Murder in the Dark, and have green goo cocktails and make pizzas shaped like dead fingers . . .' I just stared at them, planning away, being happy. How could they? I pushed my jacket potato round my plate getting cross.

'I can't wait,' George gushed. 'We're going to have the best time ever!'

Before I even knew it was happening, my mouth opened.' How can you?' I cried shoving my potato away in disgust.

'How can we what?' Millie asked, putting her forkful of pasta down, knowing very well what I was going to say.

'How can you plan and get so excited knowing Emily can't be here . . .'

'Gaby, we can't sit and be sad for the rest of our lives,' Rosie said quietly. 'Emily wouldn't want us to.'

'How do you know?' I said crossly. I felt so angry that I could feel it bubbling away in the base of my belly making my whole body shake.

'Because Emily would want us to be happy. She was a happy person,' George said in a voice implying I was stupid and didn't know anything about Emily.

'I know she was a happy person, George, I was her best friend!'

'And don't we know it?' George said huffily.

'What do you mean by that?' I asked feeling the bubbling sensation getting bigger and bigger and threatening to overtake my whole head as well.

They all looked at each other and Rosie nodded. They had prepared a speech! I was gobsmacked. 'You aren't the only person who lost a friend, Gabs,' Rosie started gently. 'She was *our* friend too. Robbie is also heartbroken if you actually bothered to notice.' Robbie— what did he know?! 'Yes, you were her best friend and you're going to feel rubbish, but you've barely spoken to us for nearly two months and every time we invite you to something you just shrug and say no. Being a tortoise isn't going to make you feel better. We *want* to see you.'

'Maybe I don't want to feel better,' I sniped. They were all staring at me.

'Why wouldn't you want to feel better?' Millie asked puzzled.

'You don't get it, do you?' I snapped. But I couldn't explain what I was too scared to say. If I felt better, then I might start to forget about Emily and she was my best friend. Just at that moment, a perfect single white feather floated down from nowhere and landed on my mushed-up potato. We all stared at it; George looked around to see who could have thrown it.

'Where did that come from?' Rosie gasped. 'That's just totally freaky!' I couldn't say that I had a collection of them in my room—they kept falling on me, or appearing in the oddest of places, like the loo, or inside a packet of waffles. I was trying to ignore them as it had got to epic proportions now and I would soon be able to fill a pillow case with them if I didn't watch it. While the girls were looking at the feather I pushed my chair back and crept away, hopefully unnoticed.

'Gabs, come back . . .' Millie shouted, half-heartedly, I thought. But I could hear George tell her to leave me alone. How could I go to the party now, even if I wanted to? They all thought I was a total loser. Maybe I was, but I knew how I felt and I couldn't stop feeling it.

I ignored the girls for the rest of the day and when everyone was on the bus shouting over the noise about the party (it seemed the whole class and his wife was going), I kept my head down and zipped my lip. I got off a stop earlier than normal so I wouldn't have to walk with anyone and went straight to my room when I got in. Max and Mum were already home.

I lay on my bed and reached underneath it for my secret stash of Maltesers in an old decorated shoebox—they had become like a drug to me. Staring at the ceiling I felt like a weight was resting on my chest. Once again I wished I could fall asleep and wake when I was twenty-five and life would be peachy.

Suddenly I had the unnerving feeling that someone was in the room with me. It was such an overwhelming prickly sensation that I jumped up off the bed. 'Max, are you in here?' I asked the air. I lifted up the side of the duvet and peered into the dust balled murkiness of the under-the-bed realm. Nothing there apart from one Converse; so that's where it was. 'Max, I don't need cheering up with one of your lame tricks.' But there was nowhere else he could hide apart from inside my wardrobe and I opened it with one quick-fire movement that wouldn't have looked out of place in a kung fu movie.

Look in your dressing table mirror, a voice whispered in my head. I looked round but there was no one there. *Go on*, it said. Was that me? Should I look? So

I sat down at my old-fashioned dressing table and tilted the mirror so I could see myself. And over my right-hand shoulder was a familiar face smiling at me. Emily . . .

Happy Halloween!

'Em, is that you?' I croaked, completely shocked and stunned. I looked at her in the mirror, rubbing the dust off it to make sure, too scared to turn round in case she disappeared.

'Yabba Gabba, it's me. Who d'you think it is?' she laughed in a normal voice.

I turned round really really slowly, expecting at any moment to wake up and for it all to be one of those odd dreams I keep having. Nope, not a dream so far, it was her all right. 'Emily, what are you doing here?' I whispered. I couldn't have Mum and Max getting the men in white coats just yet.

'I came to see if you were OK.'

I looked at her. She looked exactly the same. She was wearing her baby-blue jump suit that she had worn to our birthday. She didn't look like a ghost. Not that I am a world-renowned expert on ghosts or anything. She wasn't see-through or shimmery. Apart from there was something. She did seem a bit glowy, like she had a light behind her, but not massively glowy like Christmas tree lights or anything, just sort of emanating from her all over. She looked happy. Maybe that was what it was.

'I don't think I can be OK if I can see you. Have I died as well?'

Emily giggled. 'No, silly, *I'm* the dead one.'

This was way way too weird for me, so I pinched myself to wake up. 'Ouch, you're still here! How are you here? I don't understand.'

'Well, I could see that you weren't doing so well. Did you get my messages?' I shook my head. 'The feathers?'

'Oh yes, I knew they were from you, I think.' I wanted to touch her, give her a hug.

'You can hug me if you want,' she said like she had read my mind. 'I can see what you're thinking too.' Freaky deek!

I gingerly crept to where she was standing, about two metres away, almost at the door, and put my arms around her. She felt real, warm; I think I was expecting her to be cold, like a . . . dead person would be. I shivered. She smelt of melted chocolate. Emily gave me a big squeeze. 'I've missed you,' she said in my ear. 'I've missed the Maltesers too!'

'Oh, Em, I missed you so much,' and I burst into tears and she patted my back while I snivelled into her hair, probably getting snot and tears all over it. I really had to keep the noise down as Mum might hear and think I was mad, unless she could see Em as well. I sat down on the bed and grabbed a tissue from my bedside cabinet.

'No one can see me, only you,' Emily replied. 'And it has to stay that way. No one must know about me. You can't tell anyone . . . or I won't be able to stay . . .' She looked serious. 'Look, we can talk in your head if you like. Then no one will ever know.' I nodded. Wanting to see how that was. '*So can you hear me?*' Emily said. It was like thinking, but her voice, not mine!

'*Yes! Amazing! Now we can talk about anything. Tell me what it's like being dead!*'

'*The first thing I want to talk to you about is going to George's birthday,*' Emily said, dodging my question.

'*No way, I'm not going there. I can't face everyone. Tell me about being dead first.*'

'*There's nothing to tell.*'

39

'*There must be, it's what everyone who ever met a dead person would want to know, durrr!*' I rolled my eyes like she was thick and then realized how ridiculous I sounded saying that last sentence. Like we *really* had the chance to meet dead people all the time. In the dinner queue, at the corner shop, in Topshop. They were everywhere!

Emily looked thoughtful and squinted like she was trying to think of some answers. '*Ask me something then,*' she said uncertainly.

'*Did it hurt, when you, you know, died?*'

'*I don't know.*'

'*Where did you go?*'

'*I came here, where I am now.*'

'*But where's that?*'

'*I don't know.*'

'*What's it like, where you are?*'

'*Normal. Not hot not cold.*'

'*Are you scared?*'

'*No way. It's not scary at all!*'

'*Are you happy?*'

Emily paused; there was a silence in my head when previously her answers had been like machine-gun fire.

'Yes, but . . .'

'But what?'

'*I miss you all, but it's OK because I can see you whenever I want, but it's not the same, but I'm not sad. It's nice here. Does that make sense?*' I shook my head. How could she be happy but miss people and it all be OK at the same time?

'*Don't worry about me, I am great and cool and happy.*' And she smiled at me and I believed her because she didn't look sad at all.

'*Is anyone else there?*'

She laughed at that one! '*No! Apart from Ian, the cat I had as a toddler. Remember—he got run over?*' Vaguely. '*He popped by the other day.*'

'*Can you visit famous people and see what they look like without make-up on and on the loo?*'

She shook her head. '*Maybe a bit later on I could do that,*' she said thoughtfully. '*It's not like you think. There aren't angels sitting on fluffy clouds and angelic music playing like they do in lifts, it's just . . . normal.*'

'*You're not bored then?*'

'*No way! There's no such thing as time.*'

I was getting confused; so far I had gathered things were 'normal', not scary and that it was nice and Emily was happy, no one else was there apart from Ian the cat, no Elvis, no fun like celeb spying, no harps, no fluffy clouds. What *was* there?

'*I'm sorry to disappoint you, Yabba, but one day you will know. I can't tell you more than that.*' But she had told me precisely nothing! '*Anyway, there are more pressing issues regarding a certain birthday party. You can't stay in your room for the rest of your life. I hear your thoughts—I know you want to sleep until you're twenty-five!*'

I felt stupid. Hearing it like that in my head made me look silly. '*I know, I know. But the girls all hate me now cos I've been so moody and sad. They don't want me there.*'

'*Of course they do! It'll be great, go on . . .*'

'*No, I can't. I don't know what to say to anyone. How will I be?*'

'*I'll be with you, you can talk to me.*'

'*How can I do that? What if they can see you—everyone will totally freak out.*'

'*I told you, no one else can see me apart from you. I'll prove it. Go downstairs and I'll come with you.*'

'*Really? You want me to do this?*' I really wasn't sure. Mum was so into all that beardy-weirdy stuff as she called it. I reckon she would see Emily for sure. '*OK, I'll do it.*'

I got up off the bed and opened my bedroom door and went downstairs, checking to see if Emily was behind me, she wasn't. I panicked. What if she never came back? '*I'm already in the kitchen, doughnut brain.*' I legged it in there. Mum was making tea for us. Emily was standing pretty much right next to her when I burst into the room.

'Oooh! Gaby, you scared me to death. You OK?' I nodded. 'I was just about to call you. Dinner's ready. Can you get Max?' I went through to the lounge to grab him where he was watching some dull telly programme about building robots from tin cans, or some sort of boy-like dross.

'What's for dinner Gabs?' Emily asked, not in my head this time but out loud. Right next to Mum's ear. In fact she was shouting it.

'Shhhhhhhh!' I said.

'I didn't say anything!' Mum exclaimed. She looked at me strangely. Emily started laughing.

'See, I told you no one else could see me or hear me—only you!' And she started doing the stupid dance we did when we won at something and the other person had to take it on the chin. A bit like the Running Man, if you know what that is—quite noisy as there is a lot of jumping around. I laughed at her because she looked so funny in her posh play suit pointing her finger at me in the 'I got you' fashion.

'Gaby—that's the first time I've seen you laugh for ages,' Mum said. 'But I don't know what you're laughing at!'

'Oh, nothing, was just thinking of something Emily would have done.'

'I see . . .' Mum cocked her head and looked at me again, like she was trying to work something out while simultaneously dishing up vegetable curried rice and chicken wings.

We sat down to dinner and Emily sat on the work surface behind us. 'Dinner looks yummy, Yabba Gabba. Wish I could eat it. Sadly, I can't. That's why you have to eat the world's weight in Maltesers—like my official taster!'

'Are you trying to make me fat?' I laughed at her, out loud! Oops! I forgot.

'Eh? What?' Mum asked.

'Nothing,' I mumbled. Must remember—inside my head next time! It was so hard with Emily talking out loud; it made me want to as well.

'*Tell your mum you want to go to George's party tonight.*' This time she didn't talk out loud.

'*No chance,*' I said in my head. It was hard to do this and chew at the same time!

'*I really think you need to go.*'

'Isn't it George's birthday party today?' Mum asked right on cue.

'Yep,' I mumbled, knowing what was coming next.

'Aren't you supposed to be going to her party then? She usually has a Hallowe'en one, doesn't she?'

I shuffled around in my seat feeling like the biggest, most rubbish friend on the planet. I could lie. *'Don't even think about lying,'* Emily said.

'Yes,' I squeaked.

'What time do you need dropping off then? And what are you going to wear—isn't it fancy dress?' Emily was loving it, I could tell. She was swinging her legs and they were banging on the kitchen cupboard below. 'You could go as Eeyore, the most miserable donkey ever!' she laughed out loud.

'Yeah, funny!' I automatically snapped back at her like she wasn't dead and this was all completely *normal.*

'No need to be sarky—I thought it was fancy dress, they usually are!' Once again, Mum thought I was talking to her. This was all so confusing having a three-way conversation.

'The party starts at seven,' Emily dutifully informed me. *'If you hurry with your dinner we can go back upstairs and sort you a costume. Go on!'* I looked at her and sighed one of those mega grumpy sighs when you know you haven't got a choice about anything. Mum looked at me and turned round to see what I was staring at. I really was going to have to work out some sort of system with

Emily, as at the moment, I was looking even more mental than I had been over the past month, and that was saying something!

'The party starts at seven. I'm just going upstairs to get dressed. Is that OK?' I asked Mum.

'Of course, darling. I am just so pleased you're going out.' She smiled warmly at me and I felt so bad for how worried she must have been.

Half an hour later I was downstairs dressed like a witch, pointy hat covering my embarrassing dinner-plate ears, and all from the dressing-up chest (yes we have one; Mum and Dad are tragic—they love fancy dress). Black, black, black—you can never have enough black, I think!

'You look great,' Mum said as she grabbed the car keys. Emily had disappeared again and a little knot of fear started twisting in my gut. *'I'm in the car, stop worrying,'* I heard in my head. I couldn't do this without her. Luckily Mum had bought George a present so I didn't look like a total loser.

All the way in the car I was bricking it. What if everyone ignored me? What if I didn't know what to say? What if someone else could see Emily, like they were one of those Ghost Whisperer people from the telly?

Well, you never know, do you? *'It's all going to be OK,'* Emily said and she squeezed my shoulder. She was sitting in the back, without a seatbelt! I almost said something and then realized she was already dead so if we did have an accident, she couldn't cark it twice, could she?

'We're here,' Mum said. 'Are you going to be OK, Gabs?' She looked worried all of a sudden. I hadn't been out on my own since Emily . . . died. But what Mum didn't know was that Em was right here with me. It must have seemed strange to her, to see me suddenly be all normal, sort of.

'I'm OK. I have to do this sometime, Mum. George would be so cross if I didn't go.' Earlier I couldn't have cared less about what George thought. All I could think about was eating Maltesers and feeling rubbish. I kissed Mum on the cheek and got out of the car. 'I'm dreading this,' I said out loud to Emily.

'What did you say?' Mum asked through the car window. I'd forgotten she was still there.

'See you later!'

She nodded. I *had* to stop doing that!

'Come on, let's go,' Em said.

'Are my ears showing?' I asked tentatively, always hoping they're not sticking out from my hair, making me look like Dumbo.

'*For the millionth time, your ears are fine. All ears stick out! You have long hair and a hat, no one will see anything, and if they did, what would happen?*'

I shrugged. I would curl up and die and want to stick them to my head with Blu-tack? I *hated* them. But this was a good sign. I had almost forgotten I had ears until tonight. I haven't been bothered about them once, so maybe it's good that I am bothered again? Perhaps . . .

I knocked on George's front door. I could hear lots of screaming and laughing inside. I felt sick. The door opened. 'Hello, Gaby, I didn't think you were coming,' Jake said, dressed as a vampire. I almost gasped. I hadn't spoken to Jake since the accident. And now had no idea what to say. I automatically did an ear check to see if they were poking out. I wanted to turn and run but felt a push in the small of my back and I tripped over my long dress and fell flat on my face in front of him. Great. I was going to kill Emily . . .

I HAVE BIONIC TEETH, YOU KNOW . . .

'Here, give me your hand,' Jake said and pulled me up to standing.

'Thanks,' I mumbled. I could hear Emily laughing. *'I'll get you for that,'* I said, in my head this time. I was not going to be tricked into saying anything odd out loud at this party! George and Rosie walked into the hall to see who was at the door just as Jake had pulled me up; he was still holding my hand. George clocked him holding my hand before she said anything and I yanked it away.

Jake went bright red and said, 'Good to see you, Gaby,' then slouched off wrapping his cloak around him in a dramatic fashion.

'I can't believe you're here!' George exclaimed happily. Dressed as a black cat—she looked gorgeous in her wet-look leggings and black tight vest top.

Rosie was Harry Potter. 'We didn't think you would come, not at all.' She gave me a hug.

Emily said out loud, 'See, I told you they would be pleased you turned up.'

'*Yes, yes, you're always right,*' I said in my head.

'We're just about to play apple bobbing, come on.' And George disappeared into the living room where a wall of cheesy disco music escaped through the half-open door. The normally bright blue hallway was murky and I could hardly see where I was going. The whole house appeared to be cloaked in smoky darkness, apart from spluttering jack-o'-lanterns on the mahogany occasional table by the front door and magical fairy lights twined around the banisters on the stairs. It was pretty atmospheric. George always knows how to make a place feel special. I turned round and Emily had disappeared again.

'*Chill, I'm in the living room, checking it out, looking at what's going on, thinking up a plan . . .*' Emily's voice echoed in my head. What plan was she thinking up? '*Never you mind, nosy, all will be revealed.*'

I wasn't so sure this mind-reading trick was such a good idea after all! I pushed open the door into the living room on the left and entered the party, the smell of burning candles and pizza hitting me square in the face. 'Gaby!' about ten girlie voices screeched at once. I looked blindly for Emily in the dark, panic rising in my chest. How could I get through this if she kept disappearing?

'You have to trust me, Yabba Gabba. I won't leave you! I'm here, just not showing you myself.'

Millie was dressed as a witch too and threw herself at me and gave me a big hug. Her witch's hat fell down the back of her neck and was held in place by elastic that was cutting into her throat. 'I'm so glad you're here, we were hoping you would turn up, but didn't think you would.' She shoved her hat back on her head, stuffing her floppy brown fringe under the rim so she could at least see.

A few of the other girls in our class said hi and went back to giggling about Robbie (no doubt) and whispering. Robbie was there with Jake, standing by the food table, dressed as a skeleton in a weird black-and-white outfit that could only be described as a tight jumpsuit. It was wrong on every level. His mask was pushed up on top of his head as he crammed his mouth full of pizza. He waved over at me and Jake bared his fangs. I could feel myself go red underneath my white pancake make-up. Would I now look baby pink?

'So I think you still fancy Jake then,' Emily hissed in my ear. She was standing there next to me this time, her hair tickling my ear.

'*No chance!*' I remembered to say in my head.

'Why'd you go so red you turned pink, then?' she asked loudly, hands on hip giving me the Beyoncé finger wag. I looked at her and had to laugh—even beyond the grave, she was still doing that same old finger wag.

'What you laughing at?' Millie asked, handing me a plastic beaker full of suspicious 'punch' from the witch's cauldron on the table. One sip and inner beauty and glowing complexion guaranteed. More like spots and rotten teeth with that amount of sugar. I almost spat it out. 'I know, it's horrid, isn't it? Do you want a Coke instead?' The lesser of two evils, I nodded, relieved she had forgotten I was laughing to myself. She went over to the table and poured me one out.

It seemed like the whole class was here for George's birthday. All the boys were in one half of the room drinking the toxic punch and scoffing pizza and tortilla chips, dipping them in a bowl labelled 'Bats' Blood', while the girls, some of whom were from the other classes in our year, were in the other half whispering, giggling, comparing outfits and waiting for the fun to begin. There must have been at least thirty kids.

'Come on, guys, let's play a game!' George shouted above the cheesy music. She had just brought in a huge bag of apples and that's when I noticed there was a yellow flowery baby bath on the wooden floor languishing on top of a tasteful pink Barbie plastic tablecloth. How had I not seen that? George ripped open the bag of apples and placed them carefully in the water so as not to slop it over the edge. 'So, we playing? You've got to pick up the apples in your teeth. I've got prizes for the person who gets the most apples!'

'We can have some fun here,' Emily said out loud to me, and she winked.

'Who's first?'

Rosie volunteered, as she always does, and took off her Harry Potter pointy hat and knelt down in front of the water. But try as she might, could not get a grip on an apple with her gnashers. Everyone was cheering. She gave in and stood up, wiping her face on the pink towel George offered. Her Harry Potter lightning scar had smudged across her forehead making her look like she had been punched there instead of almost brutally murdered by He-Who-Must-Not-Be-Named.

Robbie was up next. 'Watch this!' Emily laughed. He took his skeleton mask off and got down on his hands and knees in front of the bath. He tried a few times but couldn't get one; then Emily went up behind him and pushed his head under the water so his hair got soaked. He jumped up and went mad, water flying everywhere.

'Who did that?' he spluttered. We were all laughing.

'No one, you just stuck your head under the water!' George said back to him.

'I didn't! I felt you push me, or someone did!'

'Well, it must have been a ghost because it was none of us.'

'Jake—who was it—tell me.'

'Mate, no one pushed you. I'm telling you the truth. You looked like you wanted a hair wash.' George handed him a towel and he dried off, scowling at everyone, not trusting any of us. I was trying not to laugh even more than anyone else in case they noticed.

Jake had a go next. And Emily did exactly the same. He too leapt up all indignant, but he was laughing as well—I don't think I had ever seen Jake in a bad mood. 'Yeah, Rob, very funny.' And he shook his shaggy hair like a wet dog, sprinkling us all with droplets and making the girls squeal.

'I promise on my life, I didn't touch you, mate. You stuck your own head under.' Jake raised his eyebrows at him. 'There was no one there!' Robbie reiterated.

Jake looked all around the room and he rested his

eyes on me for just a bit too long and I got the fear he knew exactly what Emily was up to and that I knew everything.

'George has hired Harry Potter's invisibility cloak and got her little sister to dunk people under!' Rosie laughed.

'To prove there's no ghost, I'll have a go,' George gamely added. And she dutifully got down on her knees, still wearing her cat mask. George chased the apples all round the tub and just about got one in her mouth by ramming it up against the side of the bath and digging in her fangs. She triumphantly held the apple aloft while dripping water all down her cat outfit, mascara seeping out in rivulets from underneath her cat mask. After that a few more people had a go, but no one could get more than one.

'*Gabs, your go,*' Emily said in my head.

'*You have to be joking,*' I said. '*I'm not getting soaked. I know what your game is!*'

'*No, I promise, not that. You want to win, yes?*' she looked mischievous and was rubbing her hands together. I nodded at her. She better not dunk me.

'I'll have a go,' I said to George. And I got down on my knees after I removed the ridiculously tall black hat.

'*So here's the plan, I'll put the apples in your mouth. Let's clear the whole tub!*' Emily laughed.

'*But won't people see the huge ripples from your invisible arm in the water?*' I asked, always the doubter.

'*No! They see what they want to see. You'll be splashing so much that you won't notice a thing. Come, on, let's wipe the floor with everyone.*'

So I lowered my head down to the first apple and put my mouth around it, only for it to bob away and for me to get a mouth full of water. 'Hey!' I said out loud.

'*You got to have a proper try first,*' Emily said. '*Make it look authentic.*'

So I tried again and this time I felt the apple pop into my mouth and I bit down, easy peasy! Everyone clapped, so I did it again and Emily again popped the apple in my mouth. There must have been about twenty apples in the bath. I just kept going and people were cheering and clapping. The final apple bit the dust and I stood up, the conquering heroine, face soaked, white make-up probably sliding down my cheeks. The crowd went wild; you would have thought I'd saved twenty puppies from drowning. George handed me a gift bag with what looked like a year's supply of sweets in it. I loved sweets!

'How did you do that?' Robbie asked. 'It was impossible to get a grip. You must have bionic teeth.' While everyone was oohing and ahhing at my Olympic feat, Emily was hatching her next trick.

UP CLOSE AND PERSONAL
WITH JAKE

'So, how did you end up locked in the Harry Potter cupboard with Jake again?' Millie asked all innocently on the bus to school a week later. We'd had half term to recover from the party and its embarrassment and I was hoping people would have forgotten about it. No chance! I was sitting head bowed, hoping to avoid Jake at all costs. I could hear Emily giggling in my ear. She was perched on the seat behind observing us with amusement and waiting for Jake to get on at the next stop. So she could start the running commentary in my head and make me slip up, no doubt. She had become very mischievous since she had died. 'Er, I actually don't know,' I replied, knowing full well who

57

was responsible for the toe-curlingly embarrassing incident.

'It's Jake's stop now,' Emily leant over and whispered to me. 'Let's see what he does . . .' The bus lurched to a stop and the doors huffed open. I could feel butterflies in my tummy, but not the excited kind, the awful I'm gonna chunder kind. What if he told people what I'd said . . .? Jake got on with Robbie and they looked up the bus and Jake pulled Rob's arm and they sat down near the front instead. 'That's weird,' Emily said. 'Why aren't they sitting with you?' I shrugged, but I knew why. Emily hadn't been in the cupboard and so didn't hear what happened. She was too busy scaring everyone else.

After I'd wiped the floor with everyone in bobbing apples at the party, George had wanted to play Murder in the Dark. But instead of playing it properly with bits of paper and victims and a murderer, one of us had to be the murderer, except we didn't know who (George tapped them on the shoulder when all the lights were out) and we had to hide. It was a bit random! A bit like something we would have played at primary school, but it was secretly funny. So, the downstairs was pretty dark apart from a few jack-o'-lanterns spitting away here and there. 'Let the game begin,' George shouted in a dramatic voice and people started running here and there screaming and trying to find a way to escape the axe murderer—who was Robbie, it turned out!

'Ow, my foot!'

'Gotcha!' shouted Robbie in a madman type voice and laughed like a loon in the dark.

'That's not fair, you only got me cos I stubbed my foot,' Rosie moaned. She had to lie down on the floor and be a corpse. 'Try not to tread on me!' she shouted as I banged my foot against her head. I didn't fancy lying on the floor so I crept back into the hall.

'Over here,' Emily said sounding all helpful. 'Go in there and hide . . .' She shoved me into a tiny cramped space. I banged my head on an edge of whatever and fell on something hard and soft that shouted and moved. It was pitch-black, not even a chink of light once Em slammed the door. And locked it! I heard the latch click. What was she playing at?

'Watch it! That was my leg you just trampled on!'

'Jake . . . ?' I asked in a wavering voice. Please, dear God and all the angels, let it not be so!

'Gaby? Oh that's just great!'

'What's that supposed to mean?' I felt sick now knowing I was possibly sitting on top of Jake, in the dark, and that he'd just insulted me.

'Nothing, it didn't mean anything. Just that you're sitting on my leg and crushing the life out of it.'

'Are you saying I'm fat?'

'What? Are you mad? Just move off my leg will you?' He sounded well grumpy. I moved, trod on his other leg, fell over and landed on him properly.

'You're on top of me now, for real.' I felt his arms slip round my back and lift me over to the side where I landed gently on what felt like plastic bags, my back resting against, and this is a wild guess, the Hoover. He was pretty strong.

'Are we in the Harry Potter cupboard?'

'Yep, the one with the Hoover, mousetraps, wellies, junk and us. There's not much room so do me a favour and don't move.'

'Yes, sir!' I shuffled around in the minuscule space that I did have, trying to arrange myself in a more comfortable position, without touching Jake. Hard, and I did graze his leg, or whatever it was, and you would have thought I'd stabbed him cos he jumped a mile. 'How long do we have to stay in here?' I asked.

'You can leave any time,' he said in a sarcastic voice. I really had no idea what his problem was.

'OK, Mr Clever, you try and open the door to let me out then.'

'Just push it. It's not locked.' And he tried to kick it with his foot and it just made a dull thump against the wood. 'What's going on?'

'Emily locked it,' I said before I could stop myself.

I heard him take a sharp intake of breath, 'What? Who locked it?'

'No one, I don't know who locked it, someone must have cos it's locked and we can't get out.' Please please don't mention it again. *Please*. Where was Emily anyway, what was she doing? She would normally now, surely, come and rescue me.

'No, I heard what you said, Gaby.' We sat in silence, and it was deafening, if you know what I mean. Outside I could hear lots of crashing about and screaming and laughing. Robbie was relishing his role as an axe murderer. My witch's hat was digging into my head and I took it off.

'Sorry about Emily's death, Gaby,' he suddenly burst out with in a mad rush, breaking the uncomfortable silence that hung between us in the dark. 'We all miss her, but it must be worse for you.'

My eyes started pricking with tears and my nose started running and I thought, horror of horrors, I was about to cry, then I remembered Emily was here and I didn't need to miss her.

'It's OK, Jake. I think I am OK now. Sort of.' *Emily, where are you?* I thought in my head. I wanted to get out of the cupboard.

'*I'm here*,' she replied in my head. '*Has Jake kissed you yet?*'

'*No! Yuck! Is that why you shoved me in here? Get me out please!*'

'*I'll send George*,' she said and I knew she was gone.

I wanted to get out of there so quickly now. I heard George's voice in the kitchen. 'Game over. Lights on.' People were laughing.

'Gaby.' Jake sounded like he was going to say something I didn't want to hear.

'Uhmyes,' I said, my tummy taking a downward dip on a rollercoaster.

'I'm sorry I haven't really talked to you since Emily died.'

'That's fine. I haven't exactly been able to talk either.'

I heard the kitchen door open and footsteps in the hall, outside where we were.

'You see, Gaby, I've always—'

'George, we're in here!' I leant over and started banging furiously on the wooden door. The hall light went on and illuminated an outline of a door in a jagged fashion in front of us and before Jake could say anything else, the door opened and we were like rabbits in headlights.

'Hey, everyone, Jake and Gaby were here all along! Ooooerrrr—what were you up to in there?' And so the ridiculing started and for the second time that night I wanted to kill Emily.

'What did you talk about in the cupboard?' George wanted to know right there on the bus.

'If they did any talking!!!!' Rosie laughed.

'Nothing, and no we didn't kiss, for the millionth time!' I said exasperated and looked at Emily who was laughing—it was brill to have her here and just be there. I felt like me again, kind of.

Registration was a welcome relief from the probing but I still had to face Jake at the back. He plonked his bag on his desk and put his iPod away in it. He was totally blanking me. His ears were red though. I turned back round from talking to the girls; if he was going to ignore me, then I would ignore him . . . *Please please don't mention I said anything about Emily.* I sat down and looked at Miss Paxton who had a strange girl standing next to her.

'Settle down, Class Three, we have a new addition in our midst. This is Francesca Browning. She is joining us from today and I want you to make her feel welcome.' Francesca was shuffling awkwardly in her shoes. She looked a bit scared and I felt sorry for her, but was sure someone would look after her properly.

'Gaby, can you take Francesca round for today and show her where everything is. She can have Em—, the desk next to you.' Miss Paxton went briefly red when she realized what she'd almost said, but covered it up by picking up Francesca's bag for her and bringing it over to me and plonking it down in front of Emily.

I felt my blood boil. Emily was actually sitting there, right next to me. It was Emily's first day back at school, albeit as my secret angel that no one could see apart from me, but still, how dare she!

'*Yabba Gabba, chill. I don't mind,*' Emily said getting up and moving across the aisle to the other empty seat next to Roisin because Ellie was off sick.

'*I do, I want to hang out with you; I don't want to show this girl round school on your first day back. Dullsville. She looks posh too.*' She did, with her perfect blonde hair brushed super straight and brand-new school uniform, not from Tesco's or Sainsbury's, but some posh shop from

61

poshville. I knew I was being mean, but I was just so cross!

'Hi,' Francesca said shyly and sat down next to me.

'Hi,' I said knowing I wasn't going to like her, not one bit . . .

THE NEW GIRL

'So, this is the canteen where we have school dinners and through that door there is where you have packed lunch.' I felt like one of those tour guides on bargain bucket holidays, showing hapless tourists where to get burgers and chips instead of trying out the local delicacies. Francesca nodded politely and gripped her see-through Tupperware packed-lunch box tightly. 'Do you want to have your lunch now and then I can show you the rest of the school after?'

'OK, that would be good, thanks.' Francesca scurried after me as I pushed through the lunch queue and we barged in the door to the packed-lunch area. The girls were frantically waving and gesturing that they had saved me a seat by the window, but we were off to explore the world of packed lunches. I never went in there; I had school dinners. It was like another universe. People sat in rows in the small dingy room huddled over multi-coloured plastic boxes at the foldaway tables, packets of crisps, foil-wrapped offerings, clingfilmed limp sarnies, tired-looking apples and bruised bananas—why would you want your mum's 'can't be bothered' packed lunch when you could have curry, chips, pizza or even proper healthy food, like jacket spuds and beans? Yummerlicious. My tummy rumbled thinking of the cheese melting on top of the beans. I would grab it after Francesca had had hers if we had time. Maybe I could go and bring mine in here? Or would that be against the law? I didn't fancy finding out.

Emily was sitting at a table away from everyone else I recognized. I would have to talk to Francesca then and not be able to even have a laugh with Emily. 'Shall I go?' Em asked aloud on cue as we sat down. 'For someone who never stops talking you're not doing too well so far!'

'No!' I blurted out loud in panic, the thought of having to do small talk with Francesca seemed unbearable because she had already proved to be as open as a tightly squeezed clam. It was like she had a wall around her that made it impossible to ask anything. I didn't like being responsible for making sure someone else was OK. Why didn't she have school dinners so we could at least hang out with my friends?

'No what?' Francesca asked, looking puzzled, unpacking her box of beige food.

'No way!' I said, not sounding convinced. 'I didn't realize you liked . . . hummus.'

'I don't really, Mum just puts it in there cos she thinks I like it. I would rather have school dinners and have a baked potato and beans and cheese.' She offered me a carrot stick to dip in the hummus—I took it, even though eating hummus was like troughing wallpaper paste.

'Why don't you say you want to have school dinners then?' I asked, glad to have a conversation opener, eating the carrot and hummus; I was starving and anything would do—flea-bitten dead horse looked good right now.

'Because I don't want her to have something else to worry about. She thinks the food here will be junk and totally bad for me, so she makes me have packed lunch.'

'Why would it be junk?' I scoffed, feeling a bit uppity about the dinners I loved. What did she know?

'I don't know. Because the food at St Helen's was really nice and had won some sort of school dinner award.'

St Helen's! OMG, that was the über-posh school the other side of town on the one-way system. The one with the red-brick wall all the way round, tennis courts, proper posh wrought-iron curly-wurly school gates. It looked like Wonka's Chocolate Factory. The one with the moss-green uniform and straw boaters. No wonder I got the posh vibe from her. For sure we weren't going to be friends now! We used to stare at the girls from that school on Saturdays when we were lounging around the high street at lunchtime looking in shop windows and imagining winning the lottery so we could buy everything from the new Topshop collection. Those girls were just finishing school and waiting at bus stops or wandering round with their brown satchels and falling down socks, giggling and tossing their long blonde/brown/black/mousy hair, all looking the same in mossy green, like members of a sect. Rumour was they had to wear green towelling knickers . . .

'Why are you here then?' I asked before I could even stop myself from being rude and asking.

'You're being very nosy for someone who didn't want to do small talk,' Emily laughed, eyeing up the rest of the packed lunch. I think she missed eating.

I ignored her. I didn't want to do small talk, but I have to admit, it was a bit intriguing.

Francesca went quiet again and bit into her, what looked like, tuna and cucumber sandwich on brown bread with those annoying seeds in that get stuck in your teeth. I spend hours picking them out of my gnashers with my nails . . .

'You don't have to say,' I reassured her. After all, I knew what it was like having people ask you awkward questions you didn't want to answer.

'No, it's OK . . .' She paused and swallowed a piece of sandwich slowly. 'My dad left us a few months ago and we had to move out of our house and I had to change schools. We couldn't afford it any more.'

'Oh, I'm sorry. That must be awful. Do you have a brother or sister?' I didn't know what else to say.

'No, it's just me and Mum . . .'

I sat there, feeling a bit lost and not sure what to say next. I have Emily to help me with . . . Emily's death. I know how wrong that sentence looks, believe me.

'Hey—Yabba Gabba! We thought you were ignoring us again!' Rosie slammed herself down next to me. 'You not eating?' Not eating never even crossed Rosie's mind. Her train of thought was always what was her next meal, how long away that was and could she have a snack in the meantime.

'We got you a treat.' George smiled at me and plonked down a steaming plate of hot jacket potato, salad, beans and cheese. 'Don't let any of the packed lunchers see—there'll be a revolt and they'll try and steal it off you.' She sat down and handed me a knife and fork. Francesca just looked on, eating her sandwich, head slightly bowed.

'Girls, this is Francesca.'

Francesca looked up from under her hair and gave a watery smile.

'Hi,' everyone muttered.

'I'm Rosie,' Rosie said and then everyone else copied, following quickly with the name telling. 'What d'you think of the school so far?' Rosie continued when the girls had finished.

'Errr . . . not sure,' Francesca shrugged. How could she know? She had been here for precisely half a day. She was probably in total shock that she was in a very un-posh school where the school dinners could poison you. 'It's a bit different to where I was before.'

'Which was where?' George probed, stealing a bit of cucumber off my plate.

'St Helen's.' Deathly silence.

'Oh,' Rosie said. Various minor celebrities sent their kids there—chat-show hosts, radio DJs, and the odd TV presenter. No one knew what to say because, as I had said earlier, those girls were the butt of our jokes on a Saturday when we saw them in their gross uniform all looking like they just stepped out of a salon with their flicky-flicky hair.

No one asked why she was here and not there. No one is stupid apart from me, it seems; you must have either got expelled, or lost all your money on the horses. And I don't think the girls wanted to pry or even get involved. As a teen magazine would say: we've got enough of our own stuff to deal with . . .

'We'll see you in the playground in a bit,' Rosie said and waved at the table. The others pushed their chairs back and got up and waved also.

'Yeah, see you in a bit,' I replied. Francesca just mouthed 'bye' and rummaged around in her lunch box to see what else her health-conscious mother had placed in there.

'*That was a bit mean,*' Emily piped up in my head when they had gone and I still didn't know what to say to Francesca. '*They could have stayed a bit longer and chatted.*'

'*Well, they don't know her,*' I tried to excuse them.

'*They won't get to know her if they don't make an effort. Go on, say something . . .*'

'*No! I don't know what to say. Anyway, she's not really . . .*' I trailed off.

'*Not really what?*' Emily demanded, getting quite het up. It was hard not talking out loud when things got a bit heated.

'*She's not really . . . the type of girl I get on with.*'

'*How do you know? You haven't even tried yet. She might be really nice.*'

I hurrumphed. Francesca looked up from her lunch at my snorting. I pretended to cough to cover it up.

'*She must be feeling fed up and embarrassed coming from that ridiculously posh school and slumming it here. Make her feel better!*'

'*Why? How? What am I supposed to do? I can't make it better.*'

'*Say the first thing that comes into your head.*'

'So, did you have any famous friends at St Helen's,' I asked desperately, hoping she would say yes so we could gossip about something. But Francesca just didn't seem the gossip girl type.

She looked at me as if to say is that the best you can come up with? 'NO!' she almost shouted. 'It's not like you all think, you know. There are a lot of scholarship kids there and girls from ordinary families who just want them to get a really good education.'

'Er . . . OK, I was just asking. I'm not *that* bothered really.' That came out all wrong . . . So what sort of education did she think she would get here? I didn't want to get involved in that conversation!

'Yes, I'd noticed.' She looked at me, right in the eye, and made me blush.

Emily sat there, head in hands, shaking her head.

'Look, can you just show me where the loo is and I'll get out of your hair.'

'I wasn't being mean; I just meant I was trying to be interested when I'm not at all interested. In celebrities, I mean.' Once again I should just be quiet.

'The loo? Please.' I could see the shutters had come down and she just wanted to get away. She was standing, ramming her leftover food into her lunch box.

'If you wait I'll come with you.'

'It's OK. Eat your lunch in peace. I need to go now.'

'Oh. OK.' So I told her where the nearest loo was and said I would meet her in the playground.

'You could have handled that better, you doughnut,' Emily hissed. 'She's probably going to do a runner now and never come back.'

I shrugged, like I was really bothered. I know it was all rubbish and I was lame, etc., etc., but really, putting me in charge of a new girl was like the blind leading the blind. I don't know what Miss P was thinking of.

Emily was right, of course; Francesca didn't show in the playground a bit later and back in the form room before afternoon lessons she just sat next to me and didn't say a word. It was like she had an exclusion zone around her screaming: don't look at me, don't even think about it! The girls were pulling funny faces and trying to make me laugh after my huge cock up, and as bad timing would have it, Francesca looked up just as they were pulling particularly contortionist gurns having me in stitches. Just grrrrreat. What a fabulous start to the afternoon.

ANGEL FEATHERS AND LAMB HOTPOT

'We're off to *Half a Sixpence* rehearsals at lunch today,' Rosie announced at morning break in the playground a few days later.

'What do you mean?' I asked, feeling a bit left out, stamping my rubbishly uncosy black school shoes on the hard concrete playground to try and stop my feet freezing solid. I needed my snug fur-lined boots, but we weren't allowed to wear them to school.

'Durrrrr! The drama group we all joined at the beginning of term is doing a musical for Christmas,' Millie said as if I was a complete idiot. And to ice the cake nicely she pulled a real thicky no-brain face at me.

I can't remember anything before Emily died. I can obviously remember my mum and dad, and brother, who I am, etc., but events, no chance. I vaguely remember signing up for something. To me, it was all a blur. 'I joined too, Gabs,' Emily said. She came up behind me and hugged me to keep me warm, and weirdly I could feel it and it helped! I was overcome by the smell of Maltesers and as usual had to have one. I ferreted around in my coat pocket and managed to pull out an already open packet and stuffed a handful in my mouth before anyone noticed.

In Junior school, all of us were always in the school plays. Emily was, of course, the star. She could sing so beautifully. When she's old enough she could go in for the *X Factor*. Oh, but she's . . . dead. I keep forgetting she can't do anything any more . . . Me, Rosie, George, and Millie always had supporting roles or were in the chorus. Now we were in Big School, we had to wait bottom of the pile again, to let all the Big Talent shine through! Wouldn't want to step on anyone's toes, would we?

'So why didn't anyone tell me you were going to go for the play?'

'We tried, but you were otherwise engaged and pretty much ignoring us,' George said quietly. Oh yes. I forgot.

'So have you all got parts?'

'Yes! I have an actual speaking part. I get to have scenes with Ewan Taylor,' Rosie said excitedly. I felt a hot flush of jealousy that they would all be doing something together. 'We've been rehearsing for weeks. But you didn't notice . . .'

'We're in the chorus.' George spoke for herself and Millie. I felt so rubbish not even realizing any of this.

'Where's your shadow?' Millie asked. 'Haven't seen her since you were so welcoming to her!' she laughed.

'I don't know. She's taken to hanging out with Roisin and Ellie for the past two days. I thought I saw Alexandra try to muscle in with her and get her to join the Kool Aids, but she probably wasn't over a five on the coolometer.'

'Oh,' Millie said. Ellie and Roisin were . . . nice, if a little dull. Kept themselves to themselves. 'We thought you were going to be her new best friend and start ignoring us again! Would you have to wear green towelling knickers to be in her gang?' And she started giggling.

'What's got into them?' Emily said narkily standing next to me. I didn't say anything. I was glad Francesca had decided to branch out with some other girls. I didn't want to be 'in charge' of her any more. She still sat next to me in form room though, in Emily's seat.

'Why don't you come to the rehearsal?' George said. 'You never know, there might be something you could help out with.'

I thought about it and decided not to go. I don't know why, it just didn't feel right, not without Emily.

'*You'll have to start doing the things we would have done together at some point,*' Emily pointed out.

'*I don't have to,*' I replied in my head, feeling a bit cross. '*What if I want to start doing different things.*' What things I had no idea. I always did everything with Emily and with the girls.

'*Well, it's good to do different things,*' Emily replied as we started walking back into school for the pre-lunch lessons—Maths—oh joy! '*You never know where it may lead and who you might make friends with.*'

'*Why are you so interested in me making friends all of a sudden?*' I asked. I didn't want new friends. I just wanted my old friends and Emily. Even if they were all off doing something without me.

'*I'm not, I was just saying. Keep your wig on, potato head!*'

At dinner break, the girls speed-ate their lunch, inhaling lumps of potato and hunks of lamb like they were in the Olympic Hotpot Scoffing event. Extra points for swallowing carrots whole, especially if they were scalding hot and made you blow out candles like you were at a hundredth birthday party and then become totally blinded by watering eyes.

'Take your time!' I pleaded. 'You will give yourselves dodgy tummies and be farting all the way through the rest of the afternoon.' Emily looked on longingly at my hotpot, which was still intact on my plate, way too hot to even tackle and I wanted to enjoy it. It was the kitchen's speciality as far as we were concerned. It had been Em's fave when she was here.

I couldn't imagine never being hungry, like Emily. How could you go through life not looking forward to a completely yummerlicious fish and chip supper or chocolate brownie from the Pink Pig Café on the high street where the centre was squidgy and the outside all crispy and chocolatey and still warm from the baker's oven? How? How? How? 'I still would like to taste food,' Em said standing behind me, 'but the need to eat isn't there. Because I'm dead.' Life would be rubbish, but I keep forgetting, Emily isn't alive. And how long will she be here anyway? For ever? Until I get married and have kids and a job on telly? Will she be my secret bridesmaid? When my head starts running away with itself like this, Emily just sighs and rolls her eyes. 'Live in the moment, Yabba Gabba. Chill.'

'We're off,' Rosie said, pushing her plastic lunch chair back from the table. The canteen was packed and there weren't many spare tables. That's what happens when you rush in here early doors. The others scraped their chairs too and stood up balancing trays with empty plates in one hand and grabbing bags and coats in the other. 'See you in tutor group, Yabba.'

I nodded and started eating my lunch. Alexandra waltzed by with a few of the Kool Aids. She stage whispered to Abby, one of the Aids: 'It must be so hard to be left out of stuff. Oh, hi, Gaby, where's your new best friend, that posh girl? Whatsername?' She had a fake look of concern on her face. I wanted to punch her and was about to retaliate when Emily stopped me.

'Don't go there, Yabba. She's trying to get a rise out of you so you look bad while she'll remain calm, like she always does, and you will look like a total muppet. Her time will come. Believe me. The best thing for people like that is to be nice and ignore her. Smile at her, it will make her mad.'

So I did, and you know what, she didn't know what to do and turned on her heel, slamming her tray down on another table, even though she had been going to sit at mine. 'You know what Mum would call her?' Emily said. 'Passive Aggressive,' she concluded. Emily knew way too much now. I couldn't keep up and I was going to get her to explain when, before I knew it, the spaces vacated by the girls were being circled.

'Do you mind if I sit here?' I looked up and Francesca stared at me, her face burning. She'd obviously heard what Alex had just said. She plonked her tray down opposite me, flicking her blonde hair out of her face.

'I didn't think you were allowed school dinners,' I said, not saying yes, but what could I say? No, go away, I'm keeping this table all to myself!

'Mum's working this week, so she's not got time to make me packed lunches and won't let me do it, so she's caved.'

'Making the most of it then.' I eyed her plate: chips, pizza, beans, not a shade of green on there.

'Yes, I wouldn't be allowed this stuff at home.' She slipped a chip into her mouth, crunching the salty crispiness of it and looking like she had escaped prison. 'Mmmmm.'

I laughed at her. 'Where are your two mates?'

'Who?'

'Roisin and Ellie.'

'Packed lunches today.'

Just then two trays slammed down one side of me. 'Hey!' both Robbie and Jake said in unison. What was today? Visitation of the people I most want to avoid?

'Hey, new girl,' Jake said. 'Nice lunch.'

'Thanks,' Francesca said whilst seemingly blushing from the roots of her eyelashes to the tips of her long blonde hair.

'Whatsup,' Robbie drawled grabbing the ketchup from under my nose.

I turned round to Emily whom, I might add, ashamedly, I had forgotten about for a second in the melee. She wasn't there! *'Emily?'* No answer. *'Em?'* I felt sick. *'Where are you?'* Total silence from Em. She'd done a runner. I started swivelling my head from side to side and scanning the dinner hall.

'Are you OK?' Jake asked. 'You've gone really white and look a bit . . . mad.'

I didn't answer. I felt overwhelmed with panic. Just as I felt I was about to pass out, a single white feather floated down from the ceiling and landed in my lamb hotpot.

'Oh my God!' Francesca gasped. 'That is . . . freaky!' And she touched it, like she was going to take it, but thought better of it.

'It's just a feather,' Jake said leaning over to pick it out. He examined it like it was exhibit number one in a murder trial. 'Though it's a bit out of place in the dinner hall, isn't it, Rob?' But Rob didn't reply. He had gone red and he couldn't take his eyes off the feather. Jake craned his neck up to the ceiling to see if a stray bird or some other explanation was the answer. No one else had noticed it.

Before I could stop myself I just squeaked: 'Emily,' out loud. Ground swallow me up, how could I let Emily out of the bag again in front of Jake? They would all think I was a total freaky deek for sure. I didn't know how to get out of this one . . .

INVOLUNTARY VOLUNTEERING

'Isn't she the girl who died?' Francesca asked. I nodded. I couldn't speak; what if she never came back and that was her goodbye?

'You think it has come from her?' Francesca whispered. 'Like an angel feather?' I shrugged, then shook my head. Deny deny deny . . .

'What *are* you talking about, new girl?' Rob suddenly spat out rather forcefully.

'I have a name,' Francesca said stiffly and bit into a slice of pizza.

'I think what my caveman friend was asking, Francesca, was what do you mean by that?' Jake said, poking Robbie in the ribs. 'Emily is . . . was Gaby's best friend.'

'Well,' Francesca chewed her pizza quickly and shot me a look. What was she going to say? That she could see Emily too????? 'Some people believe that when you need some help, a guardian angel will turn up to support you and they show you they are there by leaving feathers for you as a message.'

'Why don't they just write you a note?' Robbie asked sarcastically. 'Why not send an email from cyberspace? A feather could come from anywhere.'

'Maybe angels don't have the internet,' Jake scoffed, trying to downplay Robbie's unusual bad mood.

'You may laugh, but a lot of people believe this. Maybe this feather is a present for Gaby.'

'You girls are sooooooo wacky.' Robbie put his finger against his head to accentuate the opinion that we had screw loose. 'Where would you get an insane idea like that from?' He seemed particularly crotchety about this for no apparent reason. Why did *he* care what Francesca thought?

'My mum.'

'Well, she must be as mental as you,' Robbie sneered. 'People don't come back as angels; you die you die, that's it.' He scowled harshly at her. He was being very unlike the Robbie I knew.

'I'm not saying she's not dead, or that anyone's not

dead, all I'm saying is that maybe there are such things as angels.'

'I think there are angels,' I said. They all looked at me. 'Can we stop talking about it now please?' That seemed to work. I pushed my lamb hotpot aside and got up to leave. I couldn't get out of there quick enough. I pushed past the kids in the queue blocking the door out to the corridor and headed for the playground. I ran to the spot where the girls usually waited, but of course they were at rehearsals. *'Emily, where are you? Please come back. I don't know what to do without you.'*

'Yes you do, Yabba,' said a voice behind me. I swung round and there she was. 'You were doing just fine until you realized I wasn't there.'

'How could you leave me?' I accused her. *'I didn't mean to forget about you, really I didn't.'*

'I know you didn't, and it's good you did.'

'No it isn't! I don't ever want to forget about you!'

'No one says you have to, you blue banana!' We stood there looking at each other. *'The bell's gone, let's go inside.'*

'I think this is yours,' Francesca said as I squeezed behind her to get to my seat. She placed the feather on my desk. Emily was sitting on the window ledge at the back of the classroom. Her new seat now that Francesca had stolen her place next to me.

'Thanks.' I looked at her. She smiled and it lit up her eyes and she didn't seem so . . . inaccessible. For once I thought how hard it must be for her to be at our school, where she knew no one. And double crime that she's posh and her dad left her mum. At least he didn't die though.

'*That doesn't make it any easier for her,*' Emily said in my head. '*Just because he didn't die doesn't mean she isn't feeling like you do. It's just different.*'

'*I'm not feeling anything,*' I said inside. '*I feel totally fine.*'

'*Whatever . . .*' Emily said.

The girls got back just as Miss P started calling the register.

'How were rehearsals?' I asked George as she shuffled into her seat.

'Mrs Mooney said they needed lots of help with backstage stuff: costumes, scenery, make-up.'

Humph, not as glamorous as being on stage.

'Why don't you go for it?' George asked looking hopeful.

'We'll see.' I don't think I wanted to. It would be

weird, all the girls being in the play like we used to be and then me not in it, looking on.

'Before we start today's stimulating lesson and rev up those eager brains of yours,' Mrs Mooney began speaking as soon as we had shuffled into our seats, 'I want to say something. As you know we are putting on a musical for Christmas, *Half a Sixpence*. To coincide with this we will study alongside it the book it's based on, *Kipps*, starting this week.' The whole class groaned—no one knows why, we just did because that's what's expected, isn't it?

'Enough of that, Class Three, it's a great book and it will be an interesting way to experience the differences between the play and the book when the school performs it at the end of term. One other thing, I need people to help backstage with costumes, make-up, and scenery. I particularly need artists as we don't have a huge amount of time before we perform and only half the scenery is finished.'

George nudged me in the ribs. I hissed at her to shut up. 'Go on,' she hissed back. 'You're good at art . . .'

'Aha, you are being shamed, Class Three, thank you, Francesca, what would you like to volunteer for?' I turned round to look at her going bright red.

'For scenery, I like art,' she said.

Before I knew what I was doing, my hand was going up. But I wasn't moving it . . .

'Yes, Gabriella,' Mrs Mooney questioned (she always called me by my full name), 'what do you wish to help out with?'

Emily had stood up from her window ledge and was holding my arm up. I could feel her hand round my wrist, holding it firmly. Once again I was fascinated by the way she wasn't cold to touch, like a dead person would be. Just sort of warm and real. *'Say scenery,'* Emily said in my head. *'Go on!'*

'Why are you doing this?' I said out loud by *total* mistake in my horror of being forced into this. The class tittered under its collective breath. George looked at me like I was a complete and utter escapee from Mental Case Cul-de-sac.

'Because you put your hand up . . . ?' Mrs Mooney replied sounding puzzled.

I looked at my arm like it belonged to someone else, hoping that she would forget it was there and let me off the hook. *'Em,'* I said in my head this time, *'what are you playing at?'*

'Making you do something that's good for you. If you don't do it, you'll feel so bad and left out.'

'*Maybe that's my choice!*' I said back, wishing I could shout in my head because that's what I wanted to do. Have you ever tried to shout inside your head? It's *impossible*!

She dropped my hand and sat down muttering, '*I was only trying to help . . .*'

'*Yeah, well don't . . .*' I immediately felt bad for saying that because I knew deep down inside that she was right. If I didn't volunteer, Francesca would be involved in the play, along with the girls, and I would be completely on the outside. At least I had Em though, but maybe after today she would disappear because I was so cross with her.

'*It's OK, I know you didn't mean it . . .*' Em said.

'Earth to Gabriella—I'm waiting! Hellooooo!' Mrs Mooney was waving in my face now like I was a total idiot.

I snapped out of my daze and said as clear as a bell, 'I'll help with scenery.'

'Good—you won't change your mind in the next second?' she asked cheekily.

I shook my head, though I wanted to say yes. 'Good, I want you and Francesca to come to a meeting in the art block Friday lunchtime and you can see what we want you to do.'

'I don't want you to do that again,' I said to Emily when we got in from school and went straight to my room.

'It was for your own good.' She sat on the bed look-ing sheepish. I was slumped at my desk trying to revise for a test the next day.

'But what if I don't want to do the scenery, what if I don't want to have anything to do with the school play? What if I do just want to be miserable and left out.' I knew I was being Eeyore.

Emily just looked at me and shrugged. 'You're doing it now and I bet you'll love it.'

I turned away crossly and tried to blank my mind so she couldn't see I was relieved I wasn't left out of the group and had something to do with the play.

'How are you even able to lift my hand anyway?'

'The same way I lifted apples into your mouth . . . magic.' I guess a good magician never reveals their tricks, do they? 'Anyway, why are you revising for that test?'

'Er . . . because I don't want to fail, dumbo.'

'But, Gaby, dearest Gaby, I can help you there.'

'How? Have you become best friends with Einstein on the other side?' Maths was neither of our top sub-jects. The square root of Pythagoras's potato?

'No, I just know stuff now. Trust me. Put the book down, let's go and see what's on TV.'

What was she up to? I wasn't sure I could trust her . . .

THE MATHS TEST FIASCO

Maths was first lesson. Francesca had walked into form room with Robbie and Jake. Probably because they were on the bus together. Jake and she were chatting about the Maths test. Well, I assumed they were. I couldn't think what else they could have been talking about for so long now. Robbie was trailing behind with a face like thunder. Dragging his blue Adidas bag along the floor, the black feet on the bottom scuffing the floor and leaving a trail of angry scratch.

When we got to Maths, everyone was practically groaning with dread. Not only was Maths hideous, but tests were hideous and so was the teacher, Mr Blank. He was moody, had a tendency to get cross if you didn't know the answers to random questions that he'd fire at you, if you were caught talking, or in other words, trying to get help with the problems from a friend. He also looked like he worked in a mortuary—he had a slight hunched back and always, always wore black-rimmed glasses, a tucked-in shirt that changed every day, but they were obviously worn on rotation, and the same pair of black trousers. I guess he was pretty ancient: over forty? Who knew? Who cared? Not me. He used to call me Becky before Emily died, then afterwards, he used my real name, Gaby. Everyone did after she died, it was like I'd appeared in one of those magazines that have those circle-of-shame photos, you know, where they put a ring over a celeb's sweat patch (look—these demi-gods actually have bodily functions!!!) and everyone knew who I was, that poor girl who lost her best friend outside the school gates.

Motor mouth does it again. Anyway—the test! We all sat down. I had sweaty palms as Mr Blank handed out the papers. '*Do you trust me, Yabba Gabba?*' Emily whispered in my head, perched on the window sill behind.

'*I don't know,*' I said. '*Where're the answers? How can you see them?*'

'*They're in my head,*' she replied.

'*But you're rubbish at Maths!*' I said feeling a bit flustered.

'*Not any more! I paid Mr Blank a visit last night and checked it all out.*'

'*No way! What's his house like? What's he like? Who else do you spy on?*'

'*No one, and he lives in a flat with a friend. He's not as old as you think. He plays guitar, really well, and is in a band.*'

'*What?! Mr Blank in a band? No chance!*'

'*Yes he is. Anyway, here's how it'll work. You will try and do the test; if you get stuck I'll tell you the answer.*'

'*What? I have to actually do it myself?*' I asked incredulously. I wanted to know more about the snooping, but Emily wouldn't have it.

'*Yes, come on, you've missed the start!*' I turned over the paper and started looking at the questions. As I said, Maths wasn't my strong point.

'You have an hour,' Mr Blank kindly reminded us with a look of pure pleasure on his face—he knew he was torturing us. You could almost hear the cogs turning and brains shifting gear to climb the steep gradient. I caught Rosie's eye and she pulled a face of 'please help me!' This test must be hard for her to do that—she *likes* Maths.

I felt a bit smug as I had angelic intervention. '*Get on with it, Yabba!*' Emily hissed.

I looked down at the paper; it looked like a jumble of fractions, algebra, and random sums. I could do the first three sums after a few false starts. *'Struggling, are we?'* Emily giggled looking over my shoulder. *'Oh . . . !'*

I looked up at her; she was standing in front of my desk looking down at the paper. *'What is it?'* I asked, suddenly a little pinprick of apprehension stabbing in my tummy.

'Erm . . . that isn't the test I saw him working on last night.'

'Surely you would have checked?' I pleaded.

'I did check! It said the class name on it, it was on his desk at home.'

'He must have the answers over there somewhere?' I beseeched. This was dire. I scanned the paper and willed some arithmetic to jump out at me and reveal its answers. Funnily enough this didn't happen.

'You have forty-five minutes left,' Mr Blank said, looking up from a pile of papers he was marking. George had her head down next to me, so did Rosie in front and Millie next to her. Scribbling answers. Me—I just felt my tummy flip and the pinprick of fear start splitting open into a chasm of doom. With bats flying round, misty crevasses, and beady-eyed creatures eyeballing me from the shadows.

'*Stop the drama and do what you can,*' Emily snapped. '*I'm going to see what I can see.*' I thought this was all supposed to be like magic, that Emily could do anything.

'*I'm not a magical fairy or witch or anything,*' she scoffed in my head. I can't even have a random thought without her knowing.

'*No, you can't!*' Typical, always having the last word.

There was nothing else to do but get on with it and try my best. Meanwhile Emily was up to something. Mr Blank's chair was next to the window. '*He's got the answer sheet under a folder with papers on. I can't see them!*' Emily said. '*Hmm, let's see . . .*'

I really was struggling and was going to fail and be completely humiliated in front of everyone because I would be bottom and not even bottom, scraping in there by the skin of my teeth, but bottom by a full length of strawberry shoelace. I was stuffed.

Just then Emily, out of nowhere, knocked the clock off the wall with her arm, letting it smash next to Mr Blank's desk, the glass shattering all over the front row's feet. Rosie screamed, so did Millie, Ella, and Josie. Everyone stopped what they were doing (panicking if I know most people).

'How did that happen?' Mr Blank wondered, looking a bit spooked. 'Everyone get on with the test, please,' he said, bending down to start clearing up the mess. When he was out of the way, Emily slowly pushed the main window open until a strong breeze worked its way in and ruffled the papers on his desk. A gust forced the window even wider and the papers stacked on top of the folder went flying around the room, causing a diversion. Em was able to flip up the black A4 folder, scrabbling through the papers on the desk, holding them so they didn't fly away.

'BINGO!' she shouted above the ensuing madness. She sat down on his pulled-out chair and speed-read the answers.

'Tom, will you shut the window, please?' Mr Blank shouted above the din of howling wind, screeching kids, and general chaos. Tom duly did and the noise abated somewhat. There were papers everywhere. But the answers to the test were neatly placed on his desk, just where he was sitting before the clock jumped off the wall. Mr Blank looked like he noticed this.

'*Uh-oh, he's on to me,*' Emily said sounding a bit worried.

'Class Three, what's going on here? Is one of you up to something?' Emily had scarpered and was standing behind me, a hopeful grin on her innocent looking face.

The class all shook their heads and there were several mumblings of 'No, sir . . .' Mr Blank looked at us, and the ridiculous thought must have vacated his head.

'Right, you can have an extra five minutes to make up for the disruption, but that only leaves you . . . twenty-five minutes.'

Twenty-five minutes!!! How had that gone so quickly and I had done three sums? There were fifty-seven to go. Argh!

'Because you spent too long panicking and not enough time seeing what you could do yourself!'

'Whatever!' I hated it when Em was right. *'Just help me now please!'* And for the last, what seemed like two minutes, Emily gave me the answers for all the questions I had missed (almost all of them!).

'You better not get them all right, Gaby, you wouldn't normally.'

'How about nearly all right?' Em nodded. We finished by the skin of Barbie's teeth.

'Something's niggling me though,' Em said, *'and I can't think what it is . . .'*

We all swapped papers. George marked mine and kept looking at me funnily when she kept ticking answers right. George was good at Maths, but she was getting a few wrong, and she knew I wasn't great at it. 'You got ninety-two per cent!' she said totally disbelieving. 'How did you manage that?' She had got eighty-eight per cent.

'I did proper revision . . .' I lied and looked round at Emily who was back sitting on the window sill, twiddling her thumbs and looking thoughtful, but not in a good way.

It was nearly the end of class and we now had to read out our percentages. Most people had got about sixty to seventy per cent, with a few fifties thrown in. 'Ninety-two per cent,' I said smiling. So far I was the highest.

Mr Blank stared hard at me when everyone had finished saying what they had got. He narrowed his eyes in the style of a movie villain and turned an imaginary spotlight onto my now not so sure tight-lipped face. 'Gaby, that's a pretty amazing score. How did you achieve such a high mark?'

'I revised, sir . . .'

'Really. Can I see your workings out?'

'Nooooooooo—that's the thing that was bothering me!' Em screeched loudly. 'The workings out. We should have faked those too . . .'

I felt elephants trampolining in my tummy. Yes, readers, cheating is a mug's game. What a fab way to find that out. Argh!

'Tell him it's all in your head and you just wrote them out.' So I did.

'Well perhaps you can tell me how you got the answer to question twenty-six.' Everyone was staring now, kids turning in their seats to watch the floor show: Gaby Gets a Shoeing.

'Er . . . OK, let me see.' I looked at Emily for support who was now standing in front of me; my cheeks could have lit a small town for a week. Emily looked like a rabbit in the headlights. Then she looked at George's papers, couldn't see her workings out, looked at Tom's, the class swot, couldn't see his, then gave up and ran over to Mr Blank's desk and scanned it. 'What number did you say again?' I asked, shakily, looking down at my papers.

'Twenty-six.' Rosie was staring at me with her mouth open, catching flies like only Rosie can.

'I've found it, Yabba!' Emily screamed in excitement. My palms were awash and I was wiping them on my school skirt. Sweat was pouring down my sides under my clothes and tickling as it slid down from my armpits. Nice.

Emily started to read aloud the workings out for the sum and I slowly parroted it back to the class. My voice sounded to me like it was cracking. As I said the last bit of the equation, the bell went. But nobody moved; they were waiting to see what Mr Blank said.

'Well done, Gaby. That was correct. Please show your workings out in future. We'll go over the rest of the test tomorrow and fill in the right answers where you lot got them wrong. Class dismissed.'

Emily looked like she was going to faint, I felt like I wanted to run for the hills, but my legs were made of strawberry jelly.

'That was interesting,' Millie gasped as we headed for the loos before art.

'Can we leave it?' I asked. I didn't think I was up for any more lies today. I needed to sit in a loo cubicle. I had been saved by the bell, literally!

'So, will you want me to help you with your French test next week?' Emily said cheekily when I shut the cubicle door to see her sitting on my loo.

I could have hit her . . .

Scintillating Scenery Painting

'Who's up for the sleepover tonight?' Millie asked excitedly on Friday morning before school as we launched down the steps into the main corridor. 'Mum's getting in lots of yummy snacks and chocs. And stuff to make a chocolate fondue.'

Everyone started talking animatedly about it, but I had no idea what they were talking about. 'What sleepover?'

'Didn't we say?' Millie looked puzzled. 'Maybe you weren't there. It could have been when we were in rehearsals.'

'Oh.'

'But you're invited, obviously.' Rosie butted into my thoughts of leftoutedness.

103

'I'm not sure I can come. I think Mum and Dad are taking me out to Pizza Express with Max. It's his birthday.'

'Oh, that's a shame,' George said and they carried on talking about their sleepover, how much chocolate they were going to eat, whether strawberries or melon pieces were best for the fondue.

'Don't worry,' Emily said kindly. 'There will be other times.' I nodded, but unreasonable tears stung my eyes and I smiled through them so no one would notice. I don't know why I was so upset.

I sat down in the form room next to Francesca, but I didn't want to talk. '*Why don't you ask Francesca what she's doing this weekend*,' Em asked me from her perch behind. '*You two could hang out together.*'

'*I'll hang out with you, muppet!*' I replied. I think Emily forgets that I can't hang out with her if other people are there. Not properly. Though she is always there and it's comforting when I'm with the girls to have her there, but to be honest, it's when we're on our own that we chat and mess about.

'*Well how about you ask Millie if you can come round after Pizza Express.*' That hadn't occurred to me. Something was stopping me asking things like that.

'*OK, I will*,' I said in my head. I just hoped Mum

and Dad would allow me to. So I did ask Millie and of course, the girls were pleased.

'Come on, it's time for our meeting,' Francesca said as we trailed out of Biology ready for lunch, the best time of day. My stomach was almost yelping for tuna mayo and baked potato. I had to force it to be quiet like it was a bear waiting for its bones at the zoo. The more I tried not to think of food the more I thought of it. The back of Francesca's head was starting to resemble a steaming baked potato slathered in tuna mayo . . .

The meeting was in the art block, my favourite place at school. Art was pretty much the only lesson that I didn't struggle with. Don't get me wrong, I'm not a thicky-no-brain, but school isn't high up on my list of spine-tinglingly-exciting pant-wetting things to do before you die (obviously Emily got out of that one!). Weirdly, some kids love school. They are clearly not right in the head and need to get out more. Rosie likes school, but she does need medical intervention for her constant cheery disposition and the fact that she likes Maths—so not normal.

Mrs Mooney was waiting in the sunlit front main room of the rickety old house where we have art. Our school is pretty modern with lots of glass and brick and shiny bits and bobs. But stuck at the side by the car park in a mini garden overgrown with weeds and ivy is a house that looks like it should be in a spooky fairy tale. It's all red brick, tall, and twisty and has two Gothic towers and arches and gargoyles. It's so out of place next to our school, but I love it. There is paint all over the floorboards, huge bay windows at the front where one classroom looks over the lawn up to the new school and at the back where the other room is there is an ancient chandelier with cobwebs on it and wooden panelling all along the walls (possibly with a secret passage leading to a pirate galleon). Plastered all over the walls are kids' paintings, mood boards of real artists to inspire us, and framed photos of the old Victorian school building before they knocked it down to build our new one. The art block was part of it, the old caretaker's house.

'Aha, here they are, two new recruits!' she beamed from in front of ten other slaves, opening her arms wide and beckoning us into the vast room of paint pots, paper, and chaos. And thus followed an hour of scintillating waffle about what scenes were being painted by whom and what still needed to be done. Of course I was paired with Francesca and we were given the library scene to paint. And told that we were expected to come Tuesday and Friday lunchtimes. No way!

'I can't believe we have to come here twice a week and we don't get to hang out at lunchtime,' I moaned out loud to Emily on the way back to class. Having missed lunch I was a bit delirious and forgot Francesca was tagging along with me.

'I wasn't aware we hung out at lunch at all,' Francesca replied before Emily could.

'Oh, no, I mean, yes. I thought you were someone else. Sorry.' And I didn't mean to say that bit either!

'Thanks! Who did you think I was?' Francesca looked at me and narrowed her eyes slightly like a detective looking for clues.

'George?' I said unconvincingly.

'Are you mental from lack of food or something?' she asked.

'Yes, I think so,' I said, grateful for her get-out clause question.

'You should have said. I've got a pack of crisps in my bag. Here, have them . . .' And she rummaged around and offered me the pack.

'Are you sure?' She nodded. 'Thanks. I'm starving.' And I attacked the poor pack like a vulture scavenging the dead body of a warthog or some other creature.

By the time I had scoffed the crisps we had made it back to form room and I realized that Emily was there before me as she waved from her seat on the back window ledge. I obviously *was* delirious from lack of food not to have noticed her disappearing . . .

Back in my room later on I was primping and preening ready for Pizza Express and the way more exciting sleepover that was promised afterwards. Emily was sitting on the bed twiddling her hair and staring at me. I could tell something was wrong, or bothering her. My straighteners were hot enough and I started the lengthy process of sectioning out my hair and ironing out any kinks.

'Look, there's something I meant to say earlier,' she started.

'Spit it out.'

'I'm not going to be able to make those scenery meetings twice a week.'

'What do you mean?' I asked stopping mid straighten. 'I'm not going to those scenery meetings on my own. They're twice a week and dull as death—no offence intended.' I pictured two hours of torture a week with no one to talk to, bounce jokes off to pass the time whilst painting some jolly scene from the jolly play. No chance.

'You won't be on your own, banana brain, Francesca's there. You can talk to her.'

I knew what she was doing and I didn't like it. Was she just trying to get rid of me so she could hang out with Elvis?

'For the last time, I haven't seen Elvis . . .' Emily said witheringly.

'Which proves he must still be alive then, surely,' I offered, once again hating the fact that no thought pattern was sacred. Grandpa John refused to believe the King was dead and had all sorts of theories about the FBI and the CIA spiriting him away on special covert spying business. Pity I couldn't tell him he was right.

'You and your family are *obsessed* with Elvis. Let it lie!' Emily looked sheepishly at me. 'Look, I need to be somewhere else, that's all.' Her tone told me she meant it and I couldn't win her round.

'Where? What are you doing?' I felt a bit flat. I didn't like it that I never knew where she was and what she was doing when she wasn't here. I hoped she was OK.

'Special covert angel business. It's classified.'

'I'll miss you,' I said trying not to feel put out. 'Will you meet me outside afterwards?' Ew, I sounded like a right drip catching the hint of desperation in my voice.

'Yes.' And Emily smiled kindly at me, feeling my uncertainty. 'And I am fine and totally OK when I'm not here. Please don't worry about me, I promise on my side, things are peachy. Anyway, you and Francesca can get to know each other.'

I rolled my eyes. 'Thanks a lot!' I really didn't want Emily leaving me on my own with Beardy-Weirdy Francesca for two hours a week. 'Oooh, what's that smell?' I looked in the mirror and steam was rising from the back of my head. I'd got so irate that I'd forgotten to stop straightening my hair and it was burning. 'Yuck!' I dropped the straighteners on the floor, burning my toe in the process, and tried to survey the damage. I couldn't see.

'What's the hair situation?' I asked Emily.

She looked and pulled a face. 'You might want to wear a headscarf for a few months. You've gone bald.'

'What?! You're kidding, right?'

'Yes, but it is burned.'

I stretched my hand to the back of my head and touched what should have been silky smooth barnet. It felt like barbed wire. Grrrreat! 'I'll have to tie it back now till it calms down,' I moaned.

'It's not that bad!' Em protested. 'It's just a bit frazzled. We could cut it out.'

'What!? Cut it off, are you mental?'

'Slap some wax on it and slick it back into a ponytail. No one will know.'

'But everyone will see my jug ears. I *hate* them.'

Emily rolled her eyes. 'How many times do I have to tell you, your ears are just normal. They are not the FA cup. Tom has those.' Tom is the school swot, in case you had forgotten. You could get Sky on his ears; they are big enough to have their own microclimate. I guess Em was sick of my ear paranoia. Mum wouldn't pay for them to be pinned back either. No one understood that they were massive and stuck out at an angle from my head. Why couldn't I have cute little tidy ears like Emily's that cosied up to the side of her head and didn't stick out at all? Having my hair tied back was like the biggest most hideous hairstyle I could ever have, apart from it all falling out and leaving me with a bowling-ball head.

'We're going, Gaby, get a move on!' Mum called up the stairs. I dragged a brush through my hair and dabbed a bit of hair slick shine stuff on the back, hoping the frizz would right itself.

MAJOR MAKE-OVER
PART ONE

By the time I arrived Millie's room was awash with brightly coloured overnight bags spewing their guts on the floor. Entrails of make-up, hair brushes, nail varnishes and various snacks, some opened and some still hermetically sealed, gathered in heaps at the mouth of each bag. I wasn't sure we had enough lip gloss—ha ha!

Millie's room was very cute, all white with a red polka-dot blind and red duvet cover and stripped pine floorboards. The whole house was stylish, very 'New England' as Mum would say. I have no idea what it means, but it felt like we were in a beach house.

'So, how was Pizza Express?' Rosie asked. Obsessing about food, as usual. 'What did you have?'

'Er . . . let me see, I had . . . pizza!' I rolled my eyes.

'Which one?' she said rolling her eyes back at me.

'American Hot.'

'Good choice, I would have gone for La Reine myself.' Rosie was possibly the most food-obsessed person I knew. 'We had pizza earlier.' Of course, pizza is standard fare at sleepovers. 'What snacks did you bring?' she asked looking hopeful. I upended my pink monstrosity and the maw spilled its contents. The girls dived on it like it was treasure from a pirate galleon.

Emily gazed on wistfully from her place next to me. She was here, but not here. '*You OK?*' I asked in my head. It was usually her asking me. It didn't feel right it being the other way round.

'*Yes*,' she said a bit sadly, plonking herself down on Millie's bed next to George, who did a huge shiver. '*I'm just missing my old life a tiny bit. I wish, just for ten minutes, I could come back and join in. Eat some rubbish snacks, have one of you do madwoman make-up on me, go crazy with the hair tints George brought.*'

George brought hair tints? Hmm, maybe it would cover up my frizzy, burnt hair. They are supposed to make it go glossy, or so I thought. The adverts said so.

'*I'm sorry, Em.*' I didn't know what else to say. How do you comfort a dead person? Never mind—maybe you'll come back as a pop star and have a much more fulfilling life of fun, razzle-dazzle, and frivolity second time round? And stay away from red sports cars. Nothing could really make up for the fact that Emily was dead and missing out on half the fun. *'You can help me out here though. Can't we have some fun with your Jedi mind tricks and some spooky angel stuff?'*

She shrugged and smiled. *'I guess so. Let me have a think. I don't know whether I will come back as a pop star next time, Gabs. I'm not sure how it works . . .'* I looked at her and wished I could give her a hug, but it would look like I was hugging the air and gone a bit bonkers. Nothing new there then. Emily did a shiver and shook her head. *'I'm good. Just a bit of nostalgia getting to me. Didn't mean to worry you. All perfectly normal I believe!'* And she gave me a dazzling smile to reassure me.

'Can we open the Pringles?' George asked, already ripping the clear plastic lid off the top. I nodded. It was like a feeding frenzy in a James Bond shark pool. Had anyone actually eaten pizza? I suddenly wished Emily was real too. I forget she isn't and that the girls can't see her. They would love to know she was at the sleepover, I know for sure . . .

'You can't say a word!' Emily warned. *'I know it seems like it would be the easiest thing in the world to say it because it is real to you. They will not believe you.'*

'*But what if you did some tricks and showed yourself to them?*'

'*I can't.*'

'*Why not?*'

'*Because I can't.*'

'*You could do the tricks and we could say it was you.*' I didn't want to give up. If I could say she was real, then we would be our fivesome again, like it was before. Not a threesome with me tagged on the end.

'*If you tell them I can't come back again. You already know that!*' She gave me a look that meant business. I caved in and admitted defeat. Nice try.

'So, you're not made up and you're still in your clothes!' George said, passing the Pringles round. I took a handful, crunching three at a time into my mouth, the salty vinegar flavour piercing my tongue, making my mouth water. Pringles were wrong and right at the same time. I sat on the floor amid the jumble sale mess of girl stuff. I picked out my favourite PJs, the red polka dot ones (small vest and shorts combo) and got changed, putting the tasteful cat slippers on as well. I got appreciative 'Awwws' from everyone for those.

'I knew there was something different about you, Gabs, your hair's tied back,' George commented.

'Oh yeah!' Both Rosie and Millie exclaimed.

'It looks really nice,' George said. 'Why don't you wear it like that more often?'

I didn't let on about my jug ear paranoia. 'I just don't like it like this. It's only tied back because I burned it with the irons before I went out. It's totally frazzled and awful and I can't do anything with it.'

'Let's have a look,' Rosie said. 'I bet it's not as bad as you think.'

I slipped the hair tie out of my hair and fluffed it out with my hand because the wax had made it a bit stiff.

'It's a bit frizzy but nothing too drastic,' George said. 'It's at the back so you can't see it.'

'I can feel it, though. It's dry and minging and looks different to the rest of my hair.'

'You know what you could do,' George said thoughtfully, tipping the Pringles tube out into the palm of her hand, foraging for the last salty crumbs, 'you could put the hair stuff on I brought with me. No one else wants to do it, but you could.'

'What will it do?'

'It makes your hair shiny and stops frizzy hair, whilst giving you a bit of colour.'

I was interested apart from the colour thing.

'I think you can wash it out really easily. It's just a conditioner.' George's mum was a hairdresser and

George fancied herself as a bit of an expert. She was always having new hairstyles and trying out new products for her mum. Mandy, George's mum, cut all our hair and she was really good. She cut Mum's hair too, and Emily's mum's. She comes to your house and does it and has an office at home full of boxes of tints, bleaches, dyes, treatments, etc. It wasn't the first time George had raided her mum's supplies for a sleepover. We all did hair masks at the last one.

'Yes, why don't we do it?' Rosie shrieked. 'We could really transform you; do your make-up and everything. We're all done, sort of.' Rosie looked the same apart from different coloured nails and a few curls in her hair. The other two had full make-up including glitter and lip gloss. They needed a fresh victim. 'Let's do before and after pictures and post them on Facebook.'

Emily was agreeing out loud with the girls. 'Go on, do your hair, you can always wash it out tomorrow. Have a make-over. I wish I could have one, so you have to have one for me instead!'

'OK then, let's do a mug shot and do your worst.' I grinned at the camera nervously while Rosie took a pic with her dinky camera. George then rinsed my hair in the sink in the bathroom and applied the sachet. We chose Chestnut Red. My natural hair colour is brown so it wouldn't be too drastic. 'It says leave on for twenty minutes, but because your hair is so dark, I reckon we could leave it on for longer, as it's a wash-out one, it doesn't really matter.' I trusted George; she knew what she was doing.

'You'll be fine,' Emily said. 'You'll look great with the red bits in your hair.'

While my hair was wrapped up in a plastic bag and a towel, the girls did drastic make-up; all the while Rosie snapped away at the transformation. Make-up done, toenails painted pink and purple alternately (no point doing my fingernails—they were a state from being bitten to stumps), it was time to unveil my hair and rinse the residue off. It was a bit smelly, like wee.

'Wow,' all three of them gushed in the bathroom, 'look!'

It was redder than I thought but it looked good. 'Quick rinse, rinse, I want to see!' I was excited.

Back in the bedroom, it was still pretty red. At the back where my hair had burned was slightly redder than the rest, but it didn't look burned any more. George expertly dried it and it shone beautifully and swung like a red curtain when I stood up to look in the mirror. 'Cool! I love it. Thank you!' The make-up was all shimmery and fab too. Rosie took my final pic for the after shot.

'Your mum will go mad, surely,' Emily said sitting on the bed. 'It washes out, right?'

'Yes, yes, George says it washes out, don't worry! I'll wash it before Mum comes to get me in the morning.'

JEDI MIND TRICKS GALORE

'Do you think Robbie fancies Francesca?' Rosie asked from Millie's bed, carefully placing some chocolate buttons into her mouth like they were precious. 'We could text him and find out!'

'OOOOh! That's a bit controversial,' George said. 'I didn't know you had his number!' She was getting into gossip mode and heaving herself onto her elbows next to me, almost bouncing me off the zed bed.

'He gets all gooey eyed around her,' Millie said, fanning the flames.

'He gets cross when he's around her,' I said, hoping to divert the conversation.

'Cross, how?' George asked.

'Just cross, like he finds her annoying.' I didn't want to explain the whole canteen feather thing with Francesca. I also didn't want the girls to upset Emily. She and Robbie were . . . friends.

'He might find her annoying because he fancies her,' Millie said, not making sense. 'You know, like boys pulling your hair in primary school because they like you?' I knew what she meant: boys are a bit backwards sometimes; horrid to you because they fancy you would be something boys did, just to be even more *annoying*!

'I think Jake fancies her,' I said, even though saying those words made me feel a bit sick. I *don't* fancy him, not even for a second, let's get that straight, yeah? But I had to make up a diversion.

'Naaaaah,' George said. 'Everyone knows he fancies you.'

'Everyone? Whatd'youmean?' I asked in record speed, my words falling over themselves in the race to escape my mouth.

'Gaby, he looks at you all the time,' Rosie said. 'Always a sure sign. I tried my best smile on him, best jokes, best chat, everything, and I may as well have been talking Martian.'

'You're making this up!' I said, totally unbelieving.

'*They're not,*' Emily butted into my head. '*I've been telling you for ages, but you won't listen.*'

I didn't know what to say. He was nice, and a real boy to boot, but no way. No way would he fancy me. I mean, it's me, Gaby, jug ears and stupid jokes. I used to like him before Emily, you know, but now all that seemed so . . . pointless, like a blunt pencil.

'Maybe you should give him a chance?' Millie said.

'He'll say no!' I almost shouted.

'*I think you're more scared that he might say yes,*' Emily said, ever the smart one.

'How do you know?' George said.

I didn't want a proper boyfriend. It always ends in tears, doesn't it? Look at Robbie, nursing his broken heart and he and Em weren't even proper. Everyone plunged into silence. We always talked about boys at sleepovers, usually harmless, but this was a proper conversation, too proper for my liking! Another diversion needed . . .

'Who wants to do beardy-weirdy stuff?' I said in a mysterious voice, rubbing my hands together in the manner of a true wicked witch. As with all sleepovers (is there some kind of manual?) we had just been scaring each other senseless with ghost stories before talk turned to Robbie. You must know the ones—the Urban Myth ones. Those stories that everyone swears are true and happened to their cousin's best friend on a dark and rainy night . . . The one with the couple in a broken-down car is my personal fave when the boyfriend wanders off to get help and ends up getting murdered by an axe-wielding maniac. Typical Friday night then . . .

'So, beardy-weirdy!' I clapped my hands. 'Who's up for it or do you want to go to sleep?' Huge protestations about sleep. George went to the loo, taking Rosie with her for protection from anything scary.

'*What are we going to do?*' I asked Emily as the girls busied themselves flapping.

'*Let's pretend you think you're psychic and can see things. We could do the psychic tests that we always used to do.*'

'*Can't we just do mind-reading?*' I said, knowing it would freak the girls out completely and be hilarious.

'*No, I don't do that, only with you.*' I thought about trying to convince her, but she just shot me a look that made me think otherwise. Boring . . .

Psychic tests it was then. You pair off with pencils and paper and each of you draws a simple picture: a daisy, a tree, a house etc., and the other person has to guess what it is. By the law of averages one of you will get at least one picture right. Emily and I always used to get them right because we would do secret hand signals for house, cat, etc., till everyone cottoned on and made us sit miles apart not looking at each other.

I was paired with George when she got back from the loo. *'Draw a bird,'* Emily instructed. *'George is drawing a fish; actually, maybe you should just draw the same as her and spook the life out of her.'* What a good idea.

Rosie had drawn a snake and Millie a wonky present with a big bow on top, but neither of them got the other's right.

It was George's turn. She closed her eyes and pretended to meditate. 'You have drawn a . . . dog.'

'Nope, I drew a fish.'

'But that's what I drew!' George almost shouted. She held it up for us to see. It wasn't a dissimilar fish to the one I had drawn.

'Freaky!' Millie giggled. 'You two are up to something. Let's do some more.' So I swapped and partnered Millie and George partnered Rosie.

'I think you drawing what Millie has drawn again will be the best thing so they know it's you with the "powers". Total freaksville.' So I drew what Emily told me to: a tree with curly leaves like a cloud rather than anything artistic.

George and Rosie didn't guess each other's. Then it was Millie's turn to do me. 'A . . . spade, you know for digging the garden.' How random!

'No, I did a tree.' And I held it up.

'NO way! That's exactly what I did too!'

'What's going on?' George asked. 'You're defo up to something.'

'I promise I'm not. I'm just messing about, honest.'

'Right, I'm going to sit and watch you, sit right next to you while you have to think what Rosie's drawing,' George said firmly.

'And I'll sit next to Rosie,' Millie said, equally firmly.

'*She's drawing a flower, like a daisy with lots of petals and a round centre,*' Emily reported from the bed. '*Draw something totally different.*' So I drew a cat.

Rosie thought I had drawn a house, which is weird because I nearly did draw a house, but changed my mind at the last minute. They all looked relieved when I clearly had a different drawing to Rosie as she didn't jump up having a fit.

'You've done a flower.'

'OMG!' was all Millie could say.

'She wasn't cheating,' George reported. 'I didn't see anything odd.'

'Do some more, do some more!' Rosie chanted.

'I know—we have to get stuff from downstairs and Gaby has to guess what we've got.' It was all getting a bit mad now. 'Have you got special powers?' Rosie continued, ever the one who would love to believe in Santa if she could.

'Is it a special trick, have you got magic mirrors everywhere that we just can't see?' George asked, not liking to be outdone.

'I don't know,' I replied mysteriously . . .

Before Millie could say anything George and Rosie leapt out of the room and scarpered down the stairs to start grabbing random stuff. 'No!' Millie cried, but they'd gone into the dark and were halfway down the stairs.

'What is it?' I asked.

'The burglar alarm is on. They're going to set it off. It's on sensors so will go off the minute they go into the kitchen or the living room. Mum's going to go *mental*!'

'Emily!' I said out loud by mistake, not even caring if Millie heard me right or not. She looked at me strangely and then hoofed it out of the door onto the landing flicking the light switch as an afterthought.

'*Can you stop the alarm going off?*' I asked urgently.

'I don't know where it is, but I could—' and she'd disappeared, just like that.

Downstairs I could hear rattling doors, shuffling, hissing voices and then footsteps trying to be quiet treading somewhat fearfully up the stairs.

'OMG!' Rosie said as she catapulted back into the room; she looked a bit shocked. She sat down on the bed and waited for the others. George crashed down next to me.

'I think we should wake Mum and Dad, I think someone's down there,' Millie gasped, looking frightened to death. She reached for her inhaler on the white distressed pine bedside cabinet and took a puff, calming down her rattling breathing.

'Hang on a sec,' I said, knowing full well there was no one down there. 'What happened?'

'We got downstairs,' Rosie spoke very dramatically. 'First of all I tried to go into the kitchen and at first the handle turned, and then it was like someone was on the other side stopping it, pushing it back at me so it wouldn't open. I didn't register it at first and just thought it was jammed, so George tried the living room, and the door did the same thing, she couldn't even turn the handle. Then Millie shooed us back up here because of the alarm.'

'Could your mum have locked the doors,' I said, knowing it was Emily, who had reappeared by the door showing me a thumbs up signal.

'No—there aren't locks on the doors. They never jam like that. I don't understand . . .' Millie took another puff on her inhaler. 'What should I do?'

'Let's listen at the top of the stairs and see if we can hear anything,' I suggested, hoping they would go for it.

'No way!' George almost screeched. 'What if there's a burglar creeping around with a gun or knife?'

'If there is, he will have legged it by now,' Rosie said sensibly. 'Look, guys, maybe we should wake Sarah and Mike up, we're not going to get any sleep now.'

'I don't know . . .' Millie wavered, wringing her hands. 'Mum mightn't let me have another sleepover again.'

'Surely that's better than being murdered in our beds though,' George said. 'What was that?' She suddenly swung her head round in the direction of the door. There was a noise, a scratching sound at the door and a faint moaning.

'Oh no,' Emily said to me, 'I promise that wasn't me!'

If Emily was scared, I didn't hold out much hope for the rest of us. The door started to creak open and we all took a very sharp intake of breath. I didn't dare look because a scream was already trying to escape from my lips . . .

MAJOR MAKE-OVER PART TWO

The door got stuck on a lipgloss and the moaning turned to an 'Ouch' as someone's head banged into the door mis-timing the opening. 'You woke me up!' Millie's nine-year-old brother, Milo, said and squeezed round the door, rubbing his head and eyes at the same time. My scream stuck in my throat making me cough. George slapped me on the back.

'Shut the door,' Millie hissed. 'There's someone downstairs.'

'Who?' Milo gasped, instantly looking wide awake.

'A burglar,' Rosie whispered.

'I can't hear anything, only you lot making lots of noise.'

129

'The doors to the living room and the kitchen were jammed, like someone was holding them shut.'

'No way!' I could see he was excited by the thought of this, not terrified. 'But the alarm would be going off, you doughnuts, if someone was down there.'

'Oh yeah,' Millie said, like she'd only just thought of it.

'I know what to do,' and he whizzed out of the door and down the stairs. I heard a door opening and shutting and then another. He slipped back in the room like a Ninja. 'There's no one there and the doors are both fine—opened straight away. I disabled the alarm under the stairs first before trying, of course.'

'Get you!' Rosie laughed. 'You're a right little spy kid. "I disabled the alarm." I wouldn't have a clue!'

'I make it my business to know stuff like that,' he said smugly, like only geeky little brothers can when they've spirited their older yet much cooler sisters out of the mouth of danger.

The door swung open for a second time that night and we all screamed this time, even Milo. It was just too much.

'Right, it's three in the morning! I don't want to see anyone getting up before nine a.m. tomorrow, including you, Milo. Back into bed—now!' Sarah stepped aside so he could scuttle past, all the bravado punched out of him. 'As for the rest of you, sleep now or I will have you on gardening duty tomorrow instead of eating pancakes for breakfast. Capeesh?'

'Yes,' we all chanted. I lay down in bed, grateful I could go to sleep as tiredness suddenly swamped me like a wet blanket. I could hear Emily whisper 'night, night' as I drifted off into a land of burglars flipping pancakes whilst mowing the lawn . . .

I woke to an itchy head. It really was rather irritating—it was like the time I had nits at primary school and nothing stopped the tingling and itching apart from a really good grate with my finger nails, and then only temporarily. I could still remember the smell of the All Clear shampoo and the tug of the nit comb through my egg-infested hair.

I opened one eye. George was still asleep curled up on the edge of the zed bed, one wriggle to the right and she was off the precipice. I surveyed the room; no one was awake. I scratched and scratched and it still wasn't going away. I looked down at my pillow; in the half-light of the hastily drawn curtained room it looked like I had spilled my brains on the pillowcase. Red blotches stabbed at the pink and white spotty girlie cover. 'Erk!'

I shivered and George stirred making a grunting noise like a dying person. Not that I have ever seen a dying person or indeed witnessed the death of anyone (apart from Emily), but it was how I imagined it to be.

On closer inspection it was the dye from my head—it smelt of wee again. Yuck! And then I noticed when I went in for the sniff test that there were strands of hair all over the pillow. Not a normal amount as everyone loses a bit every day, but a few too many for my liking. My head seemed to respond with more furious itching and I ferreted away at my scalp only for more hair to fall out. 'Noooooooooooo!' I yelped.

'What? What?' George leapt up from the zed bed bouncing me off the edge of it and I fell on my side, trapped between the zed bed and Millie's bed where she and Rosie also woke up with a jolt. I could see collections of dust balls lurking under the bed and a curled up sock that was mourning the loss of its other half, abandoned in the netherworld of Under the Bed.

'My hair's falling out!' I whimpered.

'Don't exaggerate!' George moaned, rubbing fists into her eyes. 'Let's have a look.'

I peeled myself off the floor and flopped on the bed next to George so she could do an inspection. It was the nit nurse all over again!

'Hmmm,' was all she would say.

'What do you mean, "hmmm",' I asked.

'It doesn't look like it's falling out from over here,' Millie said trying to be helpful.

'It's not too bad,' George started off slowly, 'but I think Mum should take a look . . .'

'Oh . . .' I said.

'It'll be fine,' Emily soothed, having made an appearance after I woke everyone up with my discovery. 'I think George is just being cautious. I mean, it's not right that your head is itching so much, is it?'

'But we're going to visit my cousins today,' I said.

'We'd better skip the pancakes then and get right over there. I'll give Mum a ring now. OK?'

I nodded, feeling a bit sick in the pit of my tummy. Somewhere deep down, I knew I shouldn't have dyed my hair. I rang Mum to ask her if she could pick me up from George's. I had to pretend I'd left something there and wanted to pick it up.

Phone calls zinged across the room like a ping-pong ball at the Table Tennis World Championships. When Sarah came in to see if we were still alive, she spat her mouthful of tea all over me. In the daylight, my hair looked much redder than it had last night. She said a swear word—naughty! 'Gabriella, your mother is going

133

to lynch me for allowing you to dye your hair. When did you guys do this?' She looked horrified.

'Last night, when you were in bed,' Millie said. 'It washes out.'

'From the smell, I would say it's pretty permanent.' Oh nooooooo.

'Georgina, how many times have I told you to ask me before raiding the hair products!' Mandy berated George whose ears were burning and she hung her head in shame. 'You took the wrong thing. If you're going to take stuff, make sure you take stuff that isn't permanent.'

'It was with the tints and the hair masks,' George retaliated half-heartedly, knowing that there was no getting out of it: she'd messed up, Big Time.

'Yes, but *I* know that they're permanent. I shouldn't be having to arrange my cupboard to make sense to a thief just in case they steal the wrong product and end up ruining someone's hair.'

'I knew it, I'll be bald!' I wailed. Emily gave me a hug.

'I'm sorry, I didn't meant to say that,' Mandy hushed me. 'I just said that for effect. We can fix it. Now come here. Right, you left the dye on for too long, G. It's burned Gaby's scalp and hair. I've a mask we can use to calm it all down and a good chop with the scissors will do the rest and stop it snapping off. And the colour?' She raised her eyebrows. 'Back to natural?'

I nodded. Mum would go mad if I came home with short, bright-red hair. Short brown hair would be less of a shock. I hoped . . . Short hair! I hadn't had short hair since I was a baby.

'*I think you'll look great*,' Emily tried to comfort me as we walked up to the bathroom and the prep started for the second transformation in less than twenty-four hours.

'*If you hadn't made me burn my hair with the straighteners, none of this would have happened!*' I seethed, suddenly overcome with the loss of my hair and the fear of my ears being public property.

'*I didn't make you do anything. I wasn't holding them, you were.*'

'*It's OK for you, you've got gorgeous long blonde hair and are so pretty and always look amazing, even if you wear a bin bag. I'm going to look a freak and everyone will laugh. No one has ever laughed at you for having stupid hair or for having comedy ears. You haven't got a clue!*'

I wanted to cry. It wasn't fair. I was going to be a laughing stock and I knew Alex would have a field day making jokes about my prison haircut. No one had short hair at school—girls had long hair, apart from the grungy kids in the years above who looked like they didn't wash and hoiked around art folders bigger than themselves.

Emily looked at me, proper hurt in her eyes. Mandy was opening packets and had plonked me down on the closed loo seat. George was making tea downstairs. *'I'm dead, Gaby. No one can laugh at me, apart from you, if you wanted. You can either see this as a disaster or as a chance to have a new look you would never have thought of before. Stop being so negative. It's just a haircut.'*

I stared back at her. I knew she was right, but I couldn't admit it. To me, it was more than just a haircut. I hid behind my hair. There was nowhere to run if I had no hair left . . . I was nothing without my hair. My face was plain and boring. I would be a nobody.

'Don't be ridiculous, you're you!' Emily said kindly. *'Just you wait and see . . .'*

'Ta-da!' Mandy sang, pleased with herself. She spun me round to the bathroom mirror. 'Your new look!'

A stranger gawped back at me, a startled look on her face. She didn't look like anyone I knew. Her hair was delicately framing her face, her eyes were large and luminous, her cheekbones jutted out giving her a cat-like appearance. It was her ears that were the biggest surprise: they did stick out but somehow, they looked OK, they fitted with the shape of her head and with the style of the hair. The hair was textured and ruffled with wax, teased into tufts here and there; the colour was dark brown and rich-looking.

'OMG!' George exclaimed. 'You look like a pop star or a model or something.'

'It's called an elfin crop, like the film star Mia Farrow—you wouldn't know who she was! Your mum will.'

'You do look truly amazing,' Emily cooed. 'I don't think you should grow your hair in a hurry!'

'What do you think?' Mandy asked me.

I turned round and faced her. 'I love it!' I squeaked and gave her a hug. My head had stopped itching as well.

FRANCESCA TELLS a WHITE LIE

Pizza, lamb hotpot, baked potato and beans with salad, macaroni cheese, spag bol, chips—

'Gabriella, did you hear what I said?' Mrs Mooney shouted across the room on Tuesday lunchtime.

I looked over at her; all I could think about was lunch because we never got time to eat before this stupid meeting and I was so hungry I could eat a cardboard box with toxic growth-inducing paint on the side. There wouldn't be anything nice left in the canteen by the time we got out of here, and it might be closed in the last five minutes of lunch break. I know I should have brought a packed lunch but I totally forgot. I really hadn't heard a thing she'd said.

'No, sorry.'

She rolled her eyes and instructed me on helping Francesca and another girl to get the massive boards that had been erected and start sketching out the library scene on them.

'I do love your hair,' Francesca said as we struggled with the boards. 'You look a lot older. And cooler.' She wasn't here on Monday for some reason and hadn't already seen my ears on show. Lots of people had been very sweet about it, but of course Alex Bennett made her usual 'Oh look, don't your ears get cold' type of snipe.

'Thanks. It's weird not having hair hanging down my face. I don't know what to do with my hands any more—I used to twiddle my hair, there's nothing there.'

'Pick your nose instead,' she replied with a deadpan face. I laughed out loud and looked around for Emily to see if she had heard; it was so like something she would have said. But I forgot she wasn't here. Mrs Mooney shushed me.

'Do you want a snack?' Francesca whispered to me a bit later as we started to draw the initial scene in pencil on the boards, copying from a printed-out design Mrs Mooney had given us.

'Yes please, I'm just too hungry and can't think.'

'I've only got chocolate I'm afraid. Didn't have time to get much else before the bus came.' She rooted around in her bag and came up with a bag of Maltesers. 'It's weird, because I never normally like these, but I got them. I must have picked them up by mistake.' She offered me the bag after sneaking two into her mouth. 'Hmmm, they're not great, a bit like Horlicks.' And she wrinkled her nose into a pig snout. 'But they're all we've got.'

I took a couple and crunched them in two goes, the sugar hitting my tummy and not really touching the sides. Was she playing a trick on me? Had she asked someone what Emily's favourite chocolate was? I felt a bit paranoid. She didn't seem the type of person to do something like that, but you never know, do you? 'Thanks,' I said as she offered me some more.

I wondered where Emily was and what she was doing and couldn't wait for her to meet me outside when this was finished and we could run to the canteen and she could moan that she missed food while I ate my lunch in record speed. 'How come you cut your hair?' Francesca interrupted my thoughts of lunch with Emily. I hoped she was OK in the ether on her own.

'I burned it with the straighteners,' I replied, not looking at her and continuing with my careful drawing, and then told her the whole story of the hair dye at the sleepover.

'Wow,' she said. 'I love sleepovers. I haven't been to one for ages, not since Dad . . . you know.'

I did feel bad for her then. Having no dad at home. I could see my dad every day, even if he was annoying and played awful music on his stereo.

'But don't you still see your friends from your old school?' I asked, wondering if she had any other friends.

Francesca went red and her ears burned, I could see them through her hair like hot coals. 'Not right now,' she said quietly snapping the point on her pencil. I got the impression that I shouldn't ask why, so I didn't.

'Oh,' was all I said as she sharpened her blunt point.

'All your friends are in the play,' Francesca eventually spoke as we concentrated on drawing with our 1B pencils. I wanted to start writing titles on the spines. Things like *Boys Smell* by S. Tinky. Maybe when we got down to the painting side of things, I could spice it up a little!

'Yes, they are.'

'Didn't you want to be in it?'

I shrugged, of course I did, but I couldn't say I didn't want to do it without Emily. I do love a bit of a singsong and the smell of the crowd and the atmosphere of the greasepaint.

I stood back and looked at what we had done so far. Just Francesca and I were painting the library, and so far it was pretty cool.

'Good work girls.' Mrs Mooney had sneaked up silently behind us. 'You better get some lunch before it's back to the grindstone. Bring a packed one on Friday please.' I looked at my watch—the time had gone so quickly and I was desperate for food.

'Have you got lunch with you?' Francesca asked. I felt like lying cos I wanted to have lunch with just Emily on my own so we could have a catch up.

'Errrr . . . ummmm . . . no,' I said grabbing my bags and getting ready to leg it out of the door and straight to the dinner hall. Please don't ask if you can come with me, please please please . . .

'Oh. Me neither.' She looked right at me. Grrrrrrrrrrrrrr. I was silent for a moment. Maybe she would say, see you later.

She didn't. It was a stand off. I felt creepy panic start in my tummy. I hadn't been this cut off from Emily since she had . . . died.

'Shall we go?' I said, not even knowing I was saying it.

'Yes, great,' and she gathered up her bag and started jamming her arms into her coat. 'We'd better hurry, the bell's going to go in five minutes.' That set me off in a frenzy—the thought of no food like the last time. Nightmare. So we ran all the way, scarves and coats flapping like bandages from an escaping mummy. We screeched to a halt outside the canteen just as the head dinner lady was shutting the door.

'Please please let us in,' Francesca begged. 'We've been helping out in the school play and we've not been able to eat. We might faint in class.' She batted her eyelashes and smiled a megawatt smile, white teeth sparkling and her eyes enormous like Bambi's when his mother has just been shot.

The dinner lady rolled her eyes. 'Go on then, you kids, I couldn't have you fainting in class now, could I? That just wouldn't do.' She stepped aside and shouted over her shoulder to hold the clear up and to let the two lovely young girls grab whatever there was left. Pizza and chips as you would have it! We ate really really quickly, not even talking, just ramming down pieces of scalding hot pizza, burning our mouths and saying 'Ow, ow, ow!' repeatedly and laughing. The bell went and we still had at least five chips each left to eat.

'Race you,' I said and we raced to the finish, chips annihilated, plates clattering as we plonked them on the collection tray, shouted our thank yous and skedaddled out of the hall and down the corridors, navigating them expertly past all the other stragglers. We made it in time, giggling as we collapsed in a heap at our desks, ready for registration.

'You've got tomato on your chin,' Francesca pointed out to me and jabbed at my face.

'You're a tomato,' I said and that set us off giggling again. I hadn't even noticed the girls behind us.

They were staring, I could feel it in the back of my head. I looked round briefly and all of them were just goggling. I smiled at them, they smiled back and then I thought: *Where's Emily?* And as if by magic a voice in my head said, '*See you in Chemistry, banana brain.*' I looked round but couldn't see her. She was probably waiting outside. I couldn't wait to see her. She had missed so much! And then I felt strange. She *had* missed so much, I hadn't really thought about her, it felt wrong. Oh. I was a bit confused. Francesca smiled at me as we got up to leave for classes and a pang of something bit me in the tummy, I wasn't sure what. Then I realized: it was guilt . . . Francesca dropped something out of her bag. Her lunch box; I could see her food inside, uneaten. I pretended I hadn't seen it as she scrabbled on the floor to hurriedly hide it back in her bag. The cheek! She tricked me into it and I didn't see Emily because of her!

THE UNFORTUNATE
EYEBALL DISSECTION

'Have you got your eyeball?' Mum shouted from the kitchen as I grabbed my bag off the banister and started jabbing my arms into my school coat.

'Yes, don't remind me, please!'

'I bet you faint, I bet you fall over face first into the eyeball and show everyone your knickers!' Max said sneakily as he rushed upstairs past Emily who was sitting on the bottom step waiting for me to leave the house. I shot him a murderous glance and he cackled all the way up to the bathroom.

'Now, remember, if you feel a bit sick, just sit down and stop doing it,' Mum said, walking into the hall from the kitchen.

'Yes, Mum, I know,' I replied, rolling my eyes.

'Don't look at me like that, Missy, I'm just gently reminding you not to try and be brave if the end result is you passing out.' She wrapped my voluminous grey fluffy scarf a million times round my neck like a python and planted a kiss on the top of my head. 'Good luck!'

'Have you got your eyeball?' Rosie asked giggling as she clambered into the space behind me when we got on the bus a bit later on.

'Yes, please shut up about the flipping eyeball!' It was lurking inside a plastic take-away box wrapped in cling film, buried at the bottom of my bag.

'*I am so glad I'm exempt from doing this today,*' Emily said with a shiver, from the aisle behind me. '*It's positively gross!*'

'So, looking forward to gouging out the pus?' George laughed as she squeezed into the seat behind without Millie.

'La la la la la la la, I'm not listening,' I said with my fingers in my ears. Yep, you guessed it, practical time in Biology. Dissecting a cow's eyeball to see where the lens is and how it all works. I think I can get on with the rest of my life without knowing any of this. It's not like I am ever going to be a doctor, a vet, or even an optician. I don't think TV critics need to know about eyes; obviously to watch telly with, but that's about it. So what's the point?

'*To advance your knowledge of all God's creatures,*' Emily said in a smarty-pants angelic voice. '*Ha!*'

'Funny how Millie chose today to be off sick,' Rosie commented slyly.

'I'm dreading this practical later,' Francesca said the minute I sat down next to her in the form room. 'I don't eat meat so I'm worried it might make me feel a bit funny.'

'You'll be fine,' I replied a bit brusquely. She was suddenly being super friendly all the time, ever since the day before yesterday when we'd had lunch together in the canteen. But I couldn't forget her lie about school dinners.

'*Come on, Yabba, give her a break,*' Emily said from Millie's seat behind me. '*She was just trying to make friends with you.*'

'But she lied,' I said.

'*So, it wasn't like she murdered an innocent puppy! She just wanted to spend time with you.*'

'But I wanted to see you,' I protested.

'So you're not worried about cutting the eye up?' Francesca asked, not getting the hint.

'Nope, it'll be a breeze. Just pretend it's a piece of cheese or something.' I wasn't even kidding myself.

*

147

'So, Class Three, have you all got scalpels and overalls on?' Miss Easton asked at the front of the classroom.

'Why do we have to wear overalls?' Rosie asked George.

'So we don't get eye pus all over us. It might explode when you cut it with the scalpel.' Robbie sneaked in from behind our row. 'Didn't you know they might explode?'

I turned round to look at him and he was laughing with Jake, being a total idiot. Jake stopped laughing the minute he saw me look at him and went red.

I was partnered with Francesca because Millie was off sick.

'It's winking at me,' she said. 'Look.' I looked, Francesca's one still had a bit of the eyelid attached to it with some lashes still intact; it did look like it was winking.

'*I can't look,*' Emily gasped. '*Don't expect me to hang around when you do the slicing. I might have to step outside for a mo.*' She was sitting the other side of me, so I was in the middle between her and Francesca.

'*Whatdoyoumean?*' I rushed out in my head. '*It's just an eyeball.*' Like that was going to stop me from possibly barfing on Francesca.

'*Exactly! It's an eyeball. There have to be some advantages* of being dead, like being let off doing vile Frankenstein experiments.'

'Don't leave me! What if I faint?' I said rather pathetically.

'I can't help you there, either, can I?' She shrugged. She was right.

'Promise you will come right back, the minute we have finished.'

'Just call and I'll be there.'

'OK,' I conceded knowing there was no point fighting this one; I didn't want to be here either. 'Where are you going to go?'

'Where d'you think? The staffroom, to get the goss!' And she disappeared in an instant, like a magic genie or something from a weird sci-fi movie.

'You OK?' Francesca asked. 'You look a bit mad.'

'Yep, I'm fine. Let's cut this baby open.'

'Class, scalpels at the ready. Now remember what I said, no stabbing, I don't want you to damage the lens. We need to look at it intact, not in slices.' Miss Easton was so matter-of-fact, like it was every day that we dissected a cow's eyeball. 'Start at the top and work down like I showed you.'

'You ready?' Francesca asked me.

I nodded, gripping my scalpel. I knew what I had to do, but doing it was another matter. 'Get a grip,' I told myself. I pointed the scalpel at the eyeball, hoping that it would cut itself open and reveal the lens all cleaned up and blood-free. Francesca had started cutting hers, so I dived in with a tentative poke. I actually had to press quite hard before the eyeball yielded and split. YUCK!!!!! I sliced down the side like Miss Easton had shown us earlier, and as the eyeball flapped open, some unappetizing yellow pus leaked into my Petri dish. NO, NO, NO!

'Gaby? Gaby? Are you OK?'

'Mmmm?'

'You've gone white.'

'Mmmmm . . .' I had gone deaf in both ears and had pins and needles down both arms. Then I hurt my knee falling off my stool.

'Gaby!' I heard someone shout. My head was banging.

'Get her on the stool and put her head between her knees,' Miss Easton barked behind me. I couldn't do anything. My legs didn't work.

Francesca and someone else got me up to sitting and put my head down.

'How do you feel?' Miss Easton asked.

'Sick,' I replied.

'There's always one,' she sighed. 'Francesca, can you take her to the sickroom for a lie down?'

'I'm OK,' I protested. I lifted up my head and felt like it was going to explode with that head-rush feeling when you stand up too quickly.

'No you're not!' Miss Easton replied. 'Anyway, I can't have you holding up the lesson any more. Go on, off to the sickroom.'

'We'll get your bags and coat,' George reassured me.

Francesca took my arm and I leant on her, not that I wanted to. My legs were doing a good impression of raspberry jelly.

'Where is the sickroom?' she asked me when we got outside the classroom. Brilliant!

'Why didn't you say you didn't know?' I said wearily.

She shrugged and looked embarrassed. 'I just wanted to help.'

I directed us there and the secretary ushered us in and I lay down on the familiar couch where I had previously passed out when Emily died. I noticed that they'd changed the bin to one without holes! To be honest, I was feeling pretty much OK now, but the thought of traipsing back to Biology where it was looking like a massacre at an optician's was not even slightly appealing.

'You can go back to class now,' I said to Francesca. 'I feel totally fine.' I was staring at the ceiling. I was just about to call Emily. We could hang out here until Double Maths.

'I'm OK here, thanks.' She smiled at me when I looked at her funnily.

'But won't you get in trouble?'

'What for? Butchering an eyeball? I think I stabbed the lens when you collapsed. You hit me with your knee when you fell off your stool.' Oh. 'Anyway, I grabbed my bag and I've got a gossip magazine with me. We could read it if you want before we go to Maths.'

She looked really cheeky and just then I forgot all about telling Emily where I was. In fact, Francesca looked a bit like Emily. In fact, Emily would have suggested the same thing.

'Here, look at this, can you believe she would wear that on the beach?' and she thrust the 'circle of shame' page under my nose so I had to sit up and look at it.

It made me laugh. I did like a sneaky peak at the world of celebs. They brightened up the day when you were feeling a bit poo. The ridiculous hair, tans, miniature dogs, etc.

'Oh no, look at her wonky lipliner. What a loser!' I laughed. 'She looks like she put it on in the dark.'

'I think I would be scared to leave the house if I was a celebrity,' Francesca said, flicking the pages. 'We had paps at school once, when some famous DJ came to visit to see if his kids could go. He was having a look round.'

'What happened?' I asked all intrigued. Nothing like that happened at Heathside.

'Oh, nothing. I was playing hockey so saw it, but he obviously thought he was the bee's knees. He got out of his posh black car and suddenly all these paps jumped out of the bushes by the gates and started snapping away. He did a few waves and walked inside. I didn't get the big idea.'

'But still, it's exciting having paps stalking outside the school gates,' I said, impressed with the story.

Francesca just shrugged. 'Not really. It seems really stupid. Did I tell you that I heard Bailey saying to Tommy that he was going to ask you out?'

'What?!' That was a total subject turnaround.

'Since you cut your hair, all the boys have gone a bit mad. Haven't you noticed?'

'How do you know all this stuff?' I asked. Who was this girl? I hadn't noticed anyone acting weird. But then I act weird, so I probably wouldn't!

'Jake talks to me on the bus.'

'Why?' I felt sick, why did I suddenly feel sick again?

And she looked up from the magazine and right at me. 'Because no one else does.'

I could feel my ears burning bright red. I didn't know what to say.

'I haven't noticed anyone going mad,' I said shiftily as a cover up.

'Oh, they all love your new hair.'

'But Jake doesn't even talk to me any more. Ever. He must hate it.'

'So you like Jake?' Francesca asked casually, flicking through her mag.

'No! OMG, no way!' I practically shouted.

Francesca looked startled. 'Sorry, I was only asking because it seemed like you did.'

'Well, I don't.' I just wanted Emily now. I felt like Francesca was fishing for information. Maybe she liked Jake and was checking I didn't. I had no idea really. *'Em, I'm in the sickroom.'* I felt bad I had chatted to Francesca for this long.

'I know.' And she was there in an instant. *'How you been getting on? I see you passed out, again. Is fainting your party trick then?'*

'Yeah, funny,' I said out loud, by mistake.

'What's funny?' Francesca asked looking totally thrown.

'Nothing . . . Funny that you thought I fancied Jake.' Snappy comeback.

'What are you doing later?' she asked rather nervously, totally changing the subject again. Just then the bell rang very very loudly outside the office, signalling the end of Biology and time for Double Maths.

'We better go to Maths,' I said, pretending I hadn't heard her question.

'*Francesca is talking to you,*' Emily said, sounding like my mum.

'*I don't want to answer her,*' I said in my head.

'*She's waiting for you to say something. It's rude!*' Emily chided me.

'*Mum! Zip it!*'

Emily stood with her hands on her hips and her eyebrows arched. '*Answer her or I will disappear for ever.*' I knew she meant it as well.

'I'm going home later,' I eventually said through gritted teeth, wanting to scream at Em for making me say that. I couldn't think up a lie.

'My mum's picking me up from school if you want a lift home and you could come for tea.'

Tumbleweed just spun past as I panicked. I didn't want to go for tea. 'OK, great.' Argh!!!!!! Why did I say that? Why, why, why?

'Come on, let's go to Maths,' Francesca said, look-ing happy. 'It's so great you fainted so we missed all the blood and gore! Don't forget to ring your mum at lunchtime to see if it's OK.'

'*Thanks a lot, Em,*' I grumped. '*How do I get out of this one?*'

'Is there anything you don't like?' Francesca asked me as I sat down next to her in form room after lunch. I hadn't seen her properly since the sickroom incident and had almost forgotten about the tea invite because we had been so preoccupied with gossiping about Rosie's forthcoming birthday party this weekend. What to wear, who would actually turn up (would Alex and the Kool Aids try and gatecrash!!!???), and most importantly for Rosie, what we would eat!

'What do you mean?' I asked. I could think of lots of things I didn't like. Going to people's houses for tea being number one right now.

'Food wise, is there anything you don't like or eat?' Ahhh, erk. I was going to have to do this now.

'*Tell her, Gaby. Why don't you just go for tea? I'll be with you.*'

Emily was sitting in Millie's seat behind again. NO, NO, NO was all I wanted to say.

'You beat me to it,' I said to Francesca, feeling a total meanie. 'I spoke to Mum and she said Dad's coming home early tonight and we're going out for tea all together.'

'*Nice one, Yabba. Just remind her how she isn't in a family any more, and her dad isn't at home. Good work!*' Emily said sighing.

Her face fell. 'That's OK. Maybe another time.'

'Yeah, maybe . . .'

ROSIE'S BIRTHDAY PARTY

The whole class was invited to Rosie's birthday. She was having a disco in her garage at the weekend. Her older cousin Matt was a bit of a DJ and he was spinning the wheels of steel, or should I say pressing buttons on his laptop. Dad would be horrified. 'That's not proper DJ-ing,' he would grumble. 'Anyone could do that.' I couldn't!

'Hey, wow, love your top,' Rosie screeched as she opened the door, dressed head to toe in a long red and navy striped maxi dress. She looked amazing. Her mum must have straightened her wild hair. It was all swishy. I was wearing black leggings, blue denim mini, white high-top trainers and slash-neck black-and-white stripy T-shirt with a skull on the front.

'Come on, everyone's here, almost. Jake's not here yet.'

Why did she think I cared? Even so, my tummy automatically nosedived into a sea of knots.

Emily and I followed her through the house, out through the kitchen where there were several grown-ups drinking wine, down the side of the house and through a side door in the garage where it was heaving with kids. Disco lights bounced off the walls sporadically lighting up the gardening tools and the Flymo hanging precariously up on a hook. In front of the tools was a long table, covered in a white tablecloth, with piles of sandwiches, crisps, dips, cakes, biscuits, sausages and mini bottles of Coke and Sprite. For once, Rosie wasn't stationed next to it, hoovering as much food as she could. At the back, in front of Rosie's dad's work bench, was Matt, set up on another clothed table with his laptops and mixer. Ridiculously huge speakers positioned either side of him were throwing out his tunes to the excited crowd. He was DJ-ing, or cheating as Dad would say. It was so dark, apart from the disco lights, it was hard to see who was there.

I found Millie with George on the dance floor, both of them holding a bottle of drink. 'Loving the pirate look,' Millie shouted over the music. We started dancing our stupid moves and laughing. Emily was getting down too, though of course only I could see her. Rosie was bouncing this way and that, laughing with different people. The door opened and I saw Francesca come in with Ellie and Roisin. I was a bit taken aback as she looked so much like Emily for a split second, highlighted by the disco lights. She was wearing skinny jeans and a stripy batwing top. She scanned the room, saw me looking and smiled faintly but walked off with Ellie and Roisin.

'Let's get some food before it all goes,' George said and we manoeuvred through the kids and headed for the grub table. Piling our plates with goodies we traipsed over to a space where there were fewer people and sat down on some garden chairs.

'Jake's just arrived with Robbie,' Millie said, her eyes wide. I was mid-sausage at that point, Emily looking at me like she wanted to swipe it from my mouth and stuff it into her own. I stopped mid-bite, my stomach deciding for me that no more morsels were passing Go. I abandoned the sausage on my piled up paper plate.

'*Admit it, Yabba, you fancy him, admit it, admit it!*' Emily said. '*Look at the state of you, you can't even eat a poor little sausage.*'

'*I'm full,*' I lied.

'*You've hardly eaten anything. Ohhhh.*'

'*What? What?*' She went quiet and smiled at me.

'He's gone over to talk to Francesca,' said George. 'He looks pleased to see her.'

I turned round and, sure enough, he was chatting animatedly to her while Robbie looked bored. Robbie left him to it and headed over to the food table near us and started piling a flimsy plate high with crisps while eating a sausage at the same time.

'Hmm, maybe he does fancy her,' Millie said patting my arm.

I shrugged her off. 'I don't care, Millie. I don't like him anyway. She's welcome to him.'

'*It doesn't mean anything, Yabba,*' Emily said. '*He might just be being friendly.*'

'*Why won't you believe me when I say I'm not bothered?*' I sighed. '*Leave it, please!*' I wanted to storm off, but that would look like I cared, when I SO DIDN'T!! So I stuffed in the sad little sausage and it was like chewing rubber. I almost gagged trying to swallow it.

So Francesca was asking me if I liked him to work out if *she* could dive right in. She was sneaky and not being nice at all.

'*Yabba, stop it. You have no idea what she was thinking. He might not even like her. They're just talking. Anyway, why do you care? You don't even like him, do you?*'

161

Grrrrrrrrrr. Flipping mindreading! It was weird because Emily was so grown-up now she was dead! She knew stuff I could never know about and I didn't want to know about. Adult stuff!

'*Yes, adult stuff. I went on a course, you know* . . .' She looked like she was joking, but I have no idea. For all I know there are angel courses where she is.

'Uh-oh, looks like Bailey's coming over. Cancel that, Robbie and Jake are coming over . . .' George hissed.

'Girls, not dancing?' Robbie breezed in effortlessly and did a little dance to illustrate his point.

'Not like that,' George laughed. 'You've not got the moves, have you?'

'What are you saying? I can't dance? Did you hear that, Jake, G thinks I can't dance?'

'Mate, you better show her then.' He looked at me and looked away immediately.

'Come on, girls, we're dancing. Get on the floor and throw some shapes!' Robbie grabbed Millie and George and dragged them up off their garden chairs. 'Get up, Gaby, you're not let off the hook.'

I got up because the alternative was being left with Jake, and Bailey kept staring at me, and I didn't want an embarrassing moment with him if Francesca was right and he was going to ask me out. Jake followed and we barged into the other kids in the class, creating a bit of space in the middle. Lots of stupid dancing followed, and before I knew it, I was having fun. Emily was joining in too, so that was just brilliant! I even forgot about the weirdness with Jake as we all messed around laughing our heads off, Robbie and Jake taking it in turns to spin us round and round.

But then Matt decided to throw a slow dance into the mix and it all went pear-shaped.

TURNING DOWN JAKE, AGAIN . . .

'Oh no,' George groaned. 'Slow dance!' And she scarpered with Millie before I could say a word. I looked at Robbie and Jake.

'Go on, you two, have a slowie!' Robbie urged, pushing us together. 'I'm getting another sausage.'

Emily laughed out loud. 'He's playing matchmaker, Yabba! I bet Jake put him up to this!'

'What do I do, Emily? Argh!!!!!'

I looked wildly either side to see if anyone else was dancing. It was like a bomb had gone off on the dance floor and everyone had been blown to the sides, hugging the walls and making friends with the lawnmower. I caught Bailey staring aghast at us.

161

'Er . . . do you want to dance, Gaby?' Jake asked awkwardly.

'*What do I say? What do I say? What do I say?*'

'*Yes, Yabba, say yes. If you didn't want to you would have said no by now!*' Emily almost shouted at me.

'Errrr . . . no one else is. It's embarrassing.'

'OK, never mind; I'm going to get a drink.' And he sloped off to the drink table, leaving me standing there like a lemon. Just brilliant. I don't know what happened there. Yet another strange scenario with Jake that I didn't really understand. I wanted to go home. I practically ran over to the girls who had reclaimed their seats.

'What happened with Jake?' George asked. Emily was banging her fist against her head. Out of the corner of my eye I saw Bailey stride across the dance floor and go over to Francesca and ask her to dance, or so I presumed. She smiled and shook her head. He then asked Ellie, who said no, then Roisin.

'That boy is going down in flames,' Emily said sagely, shaking her head. 'Why did that guy think a slow dance would be a good idea?'

'Nothing happened,' I said, answering George's question. 'Robbie forced him into asking me for a dance, so he did. And I didn't say no, but he took it as a no and went and got a drink.'

'Did you want to dance?'

'It was way too embarrassing, and I said so.'

'I would take that as a no,' Millie said.

'I think that's a clear enough message that you don't fancy him,' George said. 'I so thought you did.'

I stayed silent. I didn't want any stray thoughts being picked up by Big Ears with the angel wings. My usual ploy of stay quiet and it might go away usually worked.

Mum turned up bang on eleven and all of us went home with her, hugging Rosie who we had a last few dances with before we left. Robbie and Jake waved as we left, but I was so embarrassed I just pretended I was looking for something in my bag and walked out.

When we got in my room, Emily sat on my bed. 'It's such a shame you blew Jake out, he's really nice.'

'Look, can you do me a favour?' I asked, tired from the party. I lay down on the bed, clothes still on.

'What?'

'Please can we stop with all the matchmaking? I don't want a new best friend; I don't want to go out with Jake. I just like this how it is.'

'But I know, really, really know, you like Jake. Even if you don't think you do.'

'So what if I do, I don't want to go out with him, OK? Let's please drop it. No more interfering.'

'OK, lip zipped.' And she pulled her fingers across her lips to jam them together.

'So, what happened at the party on Saturday?' Francesca asked when we were painting scenery on the Tuesday after Rosie's party. It was the last session before the technical rehearsal.

'You were there, nothing happened did it?' I concentrated on my painting.

'I saw you with Jake on the dance floor and then you ran off.'

'Oh, that. I didn't want to dance. I mean, who would do a slow dance, it's so tragic!'

'I know! Bailey asked me, then Ellie when I said no, then Roisin when she said no too. He wanted to make you jealous!' She was laughing. I didn't laugh back, I didn't want to chat. I didn't care about Bailey asking her to dance, I was scared she was going to ask me to come round for tea again and I didn't know if I could say no again. So I went very very quiet and just painted, hoping she would be quiet too. We had to finish it today, so the race was on.

The library did look amazing when it was finally finished about half an hour later. The books were painted in relief so they looked like real books on shelves in a dark, wooden-panelled Ye Olde Worlde book-crammed room. Francesca and I stood back and admired it, not quite taking in the fact that we had done it all on our own. I hadn't mustered up the courage to write any incriminating book titles on the spines—very disappointing, Gaby!

'You're really good at Art,' Francesca said looking at our handiwork while Mrs Mooney made us pose by the library for posterity and snapped a cheesy picture for her files.

'Thanks, so are you. I haven't really been into anything for ages. I forget how much I like doing this.'

She went quiet and then said almost inaudibly: 'You must really miss her.'

'I do,' I said automatically, as I have to say that, don't I? It was the first time she had ever really acknowledged Emily in that way.

'What was Emily like?' she asked shyly. I didn't know what to say. I didn't want to start describing Emily like she was dead and I would never see her again, because I see her every day. It was too weird.

'She's . . . was funny and pretty and had hair a bit like yours and everyone loved her.' My eyes stung. Why were they stinging? Paint fumes? I didn't want to talk about it, especially as she wasn't here. It was like I *wasn't* going to see her again, *ever*. I was suddenly gripped by resurging panic and had to leave.

'I'm going. I'll see you later,' and I grabbed my bag and various garments and headed for the door, heart in my throat, desperate to see Emily waiting under the umbrella-like pine tree at the end of the garden leading to the new school building. There was something about Francesca that made me feel . . . sad. I could see something in her eyes and I didn't want to look at it. Best not to look then and do a runner!

'We've got a technical rehearsal after school, so don't forget. Jake will be there,' Emily said as she jumped out from the majestic pine tree.

'What? How do you know? I thought we agreed no more mentioning stuff like that.'

'I didn't say he was going to be your boyfriend, did I? I just know he's going. He's behind the scenes with Robbie.'

'Have you been snooping?' I asked.

'Maybe.'

'Got any gossip?'

'None whatsoever!'

'You must if you know they are behind the scenes. I didn't.'

'You would if you listened to Mrs Mooney. She said the football team would be helping shift the scenery for the play every night and for the technical rehearsal too.'

Oh. I don't remember anything. All of the people involved in the play had to be there. In case any scenery needed tweaking or props were rubbish, etc. blah blah blah. It suddenly dawned on me that it wasn't that long till opening night with the girls on stage and I would be watching from the audience . . .

MRS MOONEY ASKS THE IMPOSSIBLE

The last week and a half came hammering towards us like a mad galloping horse with scary eyes, foaming at the mouth. Days passed in a whirlwind of school and home. Francesca and I were reduced to twice-daily brief chit-chats in form room and a friendly nod outside those times. I felt confident she wasn't going to ask me for tea again now we weren't hanging out and me and Emily were safe to hang out uninterrupted. Ellie and Roisin seemed to have taken up the slack once again. And mega-phew—there were no more awkward moments with Jake. Things were finally back to normal.

Before we knew it, it was the last night of the play. 'I think I might throw up,' Rosie said walking to the hall across the back playground. Winter had properly taken a hold now. Even last week there had been a few remaining hopeful straggling leaves clinging desperately to the branches of the trees, now all the trees were naked, arms outstretched to the unforgiving sky begging for the snow to dress them up. They would have to wait a bit longer; there was no snow just yet.

I had already been to all of the previous showings of *Half a Sixpence* as I had got roped in as a general slave after the first night when I came to support the girls. And my parents had also watched the play and oohed and ahhed at my scenery! I have to say, it did look fab on the stage.

After that night of setting out the chairs, applying make-up to the girls, doing up dresses, and general dogsbody stuff, I was asked, no *told*, I had to come back all the other nights as well! Flipping cheek. And the play was BRILLIANT! I was secretly really jealous that I hadn't been in it. '*Told you*,' Emily chided me on the night as I sat there thinking she would never know, but of course she did. She totally loved the play as well. '*I wish I was in it too*,' she said sadly. '*I sometimes miss stuff, you know* . . .' I squeezed her hand as she stood behind me, her hands on my shoulders, watching. I sneaked a look at her and her face was captivated as she bathed in the lights, the singing, the amazing dance scenes and all the first-night nerves. All things she couldn't do again for anyone to see, apart from me of course.

'So you won't want any of the snacks I've brought from home?' I asked Rosie, as we approached the outside steps leading down to the hall.

'Nope, feel properly sick. Forget butterflies fluttering in there, I've got jumbo jets taking off and landing. I need the loo again.' And she ran ahead to the toilet.

'Oh dear, Rosie is in a bad way,' I said.

'She's not been the same since she smelt Ewan Taylor's aftershave at the technical rehearsal,' Millie commented. 'She's got a monumental crush on him, but he's like *way* too old for her. He's a man!' Ewan Taylor really shouldn't work as a crush. He was in a musical (not cool, not cool), but he was monumentally good-looking (yay) so it cancelled it out. He could then have been a total dork, but everyone loved him because he was so funny, and he rode a motor bike to school and he could run rings round everyone at cross country. I could see why Rosie liked him, but he was old! Seventeen, I would suspect, so obviously people younger than sixteen weren't even on his radar. But then it's always good to have aspirations. He's a safe crush—you aren't ever going to get him, so will never feel stupid, the same as you would if he was in your class. Maybe I should try it as a hobby . . . ?

We reached the hall and Rosie eventually made an appearance. I was already setting out the chairs while chatting to Emily in my head.

'Hurry, Rosie, you've got to get your costume on before you can do make-up.' She looked green, no red, no yellow. Was she a traffic light? 'What's the matter?'

'I've just been sick and I've had a dodgy-feeling tummy since afternoon break.'

'You sure it's not nerves?'

'Look at her, it's not nerves!' Emily said aghast.

'Don't think so. I feel totally awful.' She looked like she might faint. 'I'm going to be sick again . . .' And she scarpered back to the loo. I ran after her. She was being sick when I got there and then passed out on the floor among the dregs of loo roll frayings and who knows what. I didn't want to know what if I am honest. Probably enough germs to start a new life form. It was a good job I was there.

'Go and get help,' Emily urged aloud as I tried to get her to sit up. 'I'll stay with her.' So I ran to the back of the stage where all the teachers were. There was a busy hum of activity and a comforting smell of school dinners wafting in the air (the backstage was right next to the canteen).

'Mrs Mooney, Rosie's passed out in the toilet. She keeps being sick.'

'Rhonda, can you carry on with getting the chorus ready, I've got to go.' And we ran; Mrs Mooney's bangles and earrings making a racket like a gaggle of tambourines flying loose in the back of an empty lorry.

'Is she OK?' I asked Emily out loud as we burst in the door.

'I don't know, dear, we've just got here,' Mrs Mooney replied. Doh.

Rosie was sitting with her back against the cubicle wall with the door open. Her head was in her hands. Mrs Mooney knelt down before her. 'Rosie, darling, are you OK?' She shook her head. 'Can you stand up?' She shook her head again.

'Can I just die here please?'

'I don't think you're going to die, dear.'

'I feel so ill. I don't think I've ever felt so ill in my life.'

'Oh dear. Stay there. Gabriella, stay with her, I'm going to get my phone and call her mother.'

She was back in no time, jangling like a Christmas fairy. Rosie had been sick again since Mrs Mooney had left. Rosie couldn't speak; she was shivering now and I gave her my scarf, crossing my fingers that she didn't get any sick on it. The smell of sick has a way of lingering, even after it has been bleached, nuked, or even burned off anything. 'So, Rosie, what's your number?' and she punched in the digits. I could hear it ringing and a small mouse-like voice say hello.

'Your mum will be here as soon as she can. Do you want to stay here or go to the sickroom?'

Rosie just groaned. 'I think stay here,' Mrs Mooney decided. 'Gabriella, will you stay with her? I'll go and get your other friends and let them know. I need to sort out a replacement.'

'*Poor Rosie,*' I said to Emily in my head. '*I hate being sick, it's horrid.*'

'*Something I definitely don't miss,*' Emily agreed.

Rosie was sick again and I held back her hair and my scarf, just in case. She sat back down against the cubicle wall. The drip drip of the toilet cistern was interrupted by Rosie's raspy voice. 'I know this is going to sound completely mental, but I'm going to say it anyway,' she said weakly, closing her eyes. 'When you ran off to get Mrs Mooney, I was sure I could feel someone else here. *Was* anyone else here?'

Before I could answer, the door burst open and Mrs Mooney crashed in in a comedy style, followed by George and Millie. I half expected them all to belt out one of the tunes from the play and kick off a stupendous dance routine.

'Gabriella, your friends say you know the play backwards.' George and Millie were crouching next to Rosie, stroking her back. She was pretty green, and then white around the edges.

'Yers . . .' I said uncertainly, not liking what I thought was coming.

She was talking very quickly like the words were on roller skates and didn't have their legs coordinated. 'So this is it, I need a person to replace Rosie. Kate isn't a very big part, it's just a few lines in a few scenes, but we also need that person to be in the chorus and sing as well, to know all the songs later on in the show.' She looked at me pleadingly. 'Do you feel you could do it? Sing and remember the lines?'

I felt like I was coming down with the sick bug now. Oh no, I was just about to wet my pants with nerves at the mere thought of being on stage in front of everyone and forgetting Rosie's lines, the lines that I knew so well.

'Oh, Gaby, do it, do it, do it!' Emily almost shouted and clapped. 'It will be brilliant. I can be on the stage with you and sing!'

'You could do it with your eyes shut,' Rosie croaked. 'You know the lines better than I do.'

'Come on,' begged George. 'We need you, Gaby.'

'Can't one of the chorus do it?' I asked hopefully. 'I know the lines, but not all the songs very well.'

'None of them know the lines and no one volunteered. We only have two and a half hours before we need to be ready to roll,' Mrs Mooney said. 'It doesn't matter if you don't know all the songs, just look as if you do!'

I know I had wished I was in the play after all, but it was just a wish. It wasn't meant to come true!

'Be careful what you wish for,' Emily said. Have you ever had the nightmare where you are standing on stage naked and have to recite lines? And the whole school is watching and then, horror of horrors, you end up on the toilet, *on the stage with the door open*!? No? Oh, that must be just me then. Anyway, for me, this is the same feeling of terror. Without the nakedness and the weird toilet scenario.

'O-O-K...' I managed to choke out of my shrivelled up lungs. They felt like they'd had all the air squeezed out of them very slowly by mice riding a steam roller, or so it seemed. 'I'll do it!'

Mrs Mooney clapped her hands. 'Thank you, my dear! Let's get to work.'

BLINDED bY THE LIGHtS

'Everyone, Gabriella has kindly stepped into Rosie's shoes,' Mrs Mooney broadcast across the buzzing backstage. A huge cheer went up around me, rippling through the costumes and scenery like a Mexican wave at a football stadium. 'Because this is the last night, I want to say how amazingly proud I am of all of you. So, people, break a leg tonight.' Everyone laughed and cheered at the same time. My stomach was in some kind of meltdown. Weird noises were escaping from it, a sort of secret language that only a code breaker would understand. It was probably gurgling: 'Run for the hills, you nutjob. Why did you sign us up for this?'

Emily was beside herself with excitement. *'This is your big chance, Yabba, to shine like a star!'*

'Oh my God!' I tried to shriek in my head as all around me people ran this way and that, cups of tea flying off boxes and spilling on the floor. *'What Hollywood movie are you in today? Shine like a star! You've got to be kidding me. I'll be lucky to say the lines in the right order. The only thing shining will be the sweat dripping down my face, Simon Cowell!'*

Emily was perched on a chair from the library scene. *'Listen, Gaby, I am going to be standing right behind you, or next to you, or wherever you want me to be. I know all the lines for every character, I can tell you if you need to move to the right, what to say, anything you need, I will do. I am your own private theatre director!'*

I nodded, that made me feel better. Mrs Mooney strode over to where I was supposedly studying what I was saying and doing, though nothing was going in. It was like my mind had the shutters down, was watching TV, eating popcorn and not taking calls.

'Right, Gabriella, let's do a quick run through before you get your costume on and have your make-up done.'

I found I could remember the lines from the first scene I was in. But felt I was just reciting them like a shopping list. I also had to remember the line that was the cue for the big song in the scene. Yikes. That was the one that threw me every time.

'Project, my dear, project out to the audience. They need to hear what you're saying and believe that you are who you say you are. At this moment on stage, forget Gabriella, you are Kate the snidey shop girl.'

I nodded in agreement and we went through all of it three times, where I had to stand, who else was in the scene. Mrs Mooney dragged over Matilda Rosen from Year Ten who was playing Ann, and Isabella and Eleanor who were the other two shop girls, Emma and Victoria. We walked and talked through one scene and I had to sing with them as well. Matilda had such an *X Factor* voice and I was singing like one of the no-hopers stumbling over the lines because I couldn't quite remember every single lyric, waiting for Simon Cowell to raise his hand and dismiss me with one fell blow.

'Yabba, I'll help with the lyrics. I'll shout them to you before you sing them,' Emily encouraged aloud from the wings.

'Rely on the others to carry the words if you forget the odd lyric,' Mrs Mooney offered. 'It's not the end of the world, it's not like you're singing a solo, is it?' I shook my head. 'You'll be fine, my dear!' And she swept off with her clipboard looking for someone else to point in the right direction.

George and Millie found me when I was carted off for make-up in the dingy corridor next to the canteen.

'Rosie's mum has come and taken her home. She's a complete mess. Was chattering about a mystery person being with her when you disappeared off to get help,' George recounted. 'Did she say the same thing to you?'

'Yes,' I said, wanting to lie. 'She mentioned it, but I didn't think anything of it, she was almost delirious, wasn't she?' My hair was being fiddled with by Angie, one of the older girls doing make-up, not that there was anything to fiddle with any more.

'Not quite, she was just very weak from being so sick. I wonder what on earth she's got. Food poisoning?' George asked.

'Wouldn't we all have it though? We all ate the same thing, didn't we?' Millie questioned. We had indeed eaten lamb hotpot, our favourite. We all three just shrugged.

'So, do you know what you're doing?' Millie asked nervously. 'It's so brave of you. No one else would do it.'

'What was Mrs M going to do if I'd said no then? Force someone?'

'She would have done it herself,' Angie interrupted, applying thick orange-looking pancake make-up to my entire face. 'Last year she had to play Fagin in *Oliver!* on the first night because the boy playing him got knocked out playing football that lunchtime. She's really really good!'

'Wow . . .' we all said in wonder. There was a part of me that wanted to rip off these clothes and make Mrs M step up to the mark.

'*Yabba!*' Emily said sadly next to me. '*Please don't drop out, not now we're here!*'

Then I realized, I was doing this for Emily really. Not especially for myself. I did want to be in the play, but I wanted to be in the play and have rehearsed and not feel this sick dread trying hard to escape from my insides. This wasn't how I wanted it. But I would do it for Emily. '*I'm here till the end,*' I sighed inside.

Before I could even say 'I'm not ready', I was ready. I was wearing a long, full navy-blue skirt with a white high-necked blouse that was choking me and my hair was all combed forward with a narrow white Alice band plonked in the middle of my head. I looked very prim. The total shock was the make-up. Kohl-rimmed eyes pencilled on in a thick line, rosy cheeks, vaguely orange skin—I looked like one of those 'circle of shame' celebs in a magazine, spotted out with wrong make-up! I almost screamed. 'Yep, it's always a bit weird when you see yourself in the "mask" for the first time,' Angie said, laughing at my anguished face in the hand-held mirror she proffered me. 'It has to be like this because of the lights. Your features will just disappear on stage otherwise.'

'Twenty minutes till curtain,' Mrs Mooney announced continually in a hushed tone as she alerted us all backstage and out in the corridor. The audience was arriving. The thick maroon velvet stage curtains were shut now. Backstage had been cut off by the black solid curtain sealing everyone in there with the chaos while the stage was clear and serene. Everything was in place; the opening scene of Shalford's Emporium was set with a long wooden bench, stolen from the woodwork department, centre stage, and on top of it an old-fashioned till perched at one end. Scenery painted with careful detail showing bolts and bolts of colourful material for fashioning men's shirts and ladies' blouses and more sober material for making the suits. I felt like I was in the shop for real. There were signs pointing this way and that to the Glove Department or Ladies' Coats.

Emily was singing the song 'I Don't Believe a Word of It' to me so I could absorb the words amid the last-minute scufflings and shufflings.

The orchestra was warming up. I saw Jake and Robbie clothed in black from head to toe leaning against a piece of scenery in the opposite wings. Mrs Mooney scuttled over to Jake and whispered something in his ear. He leapt up and ran over to the side of the stage I was on. 'Excuse me, Gaby, you're standing in front of the brush. I need it.'

'Oh. Sorry.' I stepped aside so he could reach it. It was the first time he had spoken directly to me for weeks, having ignored me after the slow dance disaster at Rosie's party.

'Good luck, I mean break a leg,' he stammered.

'Thanks, I think . . .' And he rushed off with his brush and started to sweep the stage, making it super-clean ready for action.

George and Millie came over: 'Come and do the voice warm-ups with us in the corridor.' Emily followed, wanting to be in the thick of it. Ewan Taylor was leading the warm up with the whole cast crammed into the corridor at the side of the backstage area. The cast were squashed up against a pinboard of art work from Year Nine students. The girls kept unhooking their hair from the drawing pins holding the still life paintings on display. It was just so rammed.

'Aha, our saviour, Gaby. Come and get warmed up before your debut.'

'Er . . . er . . . hi . . .' I could barely speak. It was as if I had suddenly been allowed to join the Popular Club. Ewan Taylor was speaking to me, *me*, Gaby Richards. I was the only person mentioned in that hallowed sentence. I felt like I had won the lottery. He was so hot I couldn't look directly at him for fear of burning up, even when I knew he was smiling at me. Durrrr. George poked me in the back because she knew I would be wetting myself about it!

Ewan took us through the scales and some, quite frankly, ridiculous-sounding vocal exercises! Emily was doing them even though she wasn't in the play.

I really couldn't believe we were here, the last night of *Half a Sixpence*. After all the scenery painting, prop making, line learning on the bus, it didn't seem real. I hadn't liked the book, *Kipps*, when we had it read it in class because the cockney-sounding language was difficult to understand and I did have to endure a few lessons of sleep with eyes open, but the play breathed life into the characters of Arty and Ann.

Arty and Ann are two childhood friends, who split an old silver sixpence in half and keep one half each. They become old-fashioned 'sweethearts'. But one day Arty inherits a fortune, forgets his old sweetheart, runs off with a mega-posh older lady, almost marries her, gets all la-di-da, totally makes a huge mistake, regrets it, begs Ann to marry him, they get married and then posh lady's brother embezzles all his money, so he's just normal again. But happy. And the message, ladies and gentlemen is: don't overlook what's right under your nose because that's probably just what you're looking for . . . !

'Five minutes! Five minutes!' Robbie called down the corridor. We all hurried up the two narrow wooden stairs to the backstage and bustled through the door, skirts getting caught. Ewan and chorus shop boys and girls were on the stage. I wasn't in this bit of the chorus. George and Millie were though, dressed in long black skirts and white, frilly high-necked blouses, their hair piled high and pinned in meringues on their heads. I had to come on during the opening scene a few minutes in.

The orchestra started playing the overture. The curtain went up and the magic began. I was in the wings ready to go on as Kate, the shop girl, carrying a bundle of cloth towards the counter. I felt like I was encased in cardboard in my starched blouse and was soaked with sweat.

I peered over the footlights and out into the audience, trying to see if there was anyone I knew. '*Don't look!*' Emily hissed in my head from behind me. '*It will just make you nervous. Imagine it's just you and me in your bedroom messing about.'* Too late, I'd seen Francesca about three rows back with a blonde-haired woman who must be her mum. I couldn't see her dad anywhere, but then I wouldn't know what he looked like. He wasn't sitting with them, anyway. I couldn't see much more than that because the lights were too bright.

'You're on,' Andie the stage manager whispered and pushed me forwards after the opening number finished. I skidded a bit on the floor under my long skirts and felt a cold bead of sweat trickle down both sides of my body. The lights were blinding and I stupidly looked at one and was, for about ten seconds, totally and utterly blinded.

'*Stop walking,*' Emily urged. She was right beside me. '*No one has noticed. They're all watching Ewan centre stage. You have to go and put that material on the counter now, I'll guide you,*' and she took my arm from behind and made me walk towards the wooden desk where I had to engage in fake chatting with the girl on the till and turn to my right and show a lady customer the material. '*Turn to your left slightly,*' Em said. My eyes were watering from the lights so that I wanted to wipe them. '*Don't even think about it,*' she hissed. '*You'll end up with make-up all over your gloves and black smears all down your face. Man up!*'

Man up? Flipping heck. I had only just walked on to stage, not even had to utter a word and so far everything was going totally down the plughole. How was I going to get through the rest of the play? Thank the Lord that Emily was here.

THE SHOW MUST GO ON

The rest of the scene was just about OK. Ewan was singing 'Economy' with the chorus like a livewire. I was the opposite—the energy it took to remember the lyrics, and the concentration it took to follow the girls on stage was draining me. I didn't have any extra chutzpah! By then my eyes had cleared up and the sweat factory in my armpits was on dinner break, for now. By the time it was scenery change, I was ready to collapse. We all scurried off stage after the black-out curtain came down, while behind it Robbie, Jake, and the football team hefted the big pieces of scenery from one side to the other, all traces of the shop gone and the promenade scene magically appearing in its place.

As Ewan and Matilda were singing 'Half a Sixpence', we downed some water, had our faces patted with powder to stop the shine and waited to go on. Mrs Mooney came over to where I was standing with Eleanor and Isabella, the other two shop girls. 'Good going, Gabriella. A bit wobbly at first but you pulled it out of the bag in the end. Just try and enjoy it and don't look so scared!'

Easier said than done, Mrs M, I thought.

'*Rely on me*,' Emily said. '*I'm here if you need me. I obviously can't tell you how to dance though—that's all your doing.*' I'm not known for my dancing. An octopus trying to put on tights would describe it rather well. Give me Abba any day, but actual sequenced dancing—no chance. My brain knows what my legs need to do, but somehow the signal gets confused along the way. Maybe it thinks my legs should be attempting breakdancing, or whatever, and the original message of 'put one foot here and the other foot there' is lost. Out comes another step altogether, mimicking the octopus.

It was like the Hand of Fate, or some invisible busybody, had got their finger on the fast-forward button. Just as I felt like I had five minutes to go through the song lyrics, Emily shouted: 'This is it, Yabba, we're on . . .' Emily was as excited as I was nervous. I had one key line that wasn't just the banter with the other

191

girls, it led on to the big musical number we had to sing as a group. I kept saying it over and over in my head because the other lines were easy to remember, but this one was a cue for Ann's song. And there was a weird word at the end of it: philandering. I had never heard it before Rosie got the part of Kate. It describes a man who keeps having different girlfriends, one after another, possibly behind the others' backs! Nice.

'Good luck, Gaby,' Eleanor said and squeezed my hand. 'I'll guide you where to follow so just go with it. You're doing really well.' Isabella nodded and smiled. She looked nervous, probably bricking it that I was going to totally ruin their big scene and somehow it would all be her fault!

We walked onto the stage behind the blackout curtain. I could see Jake in the wings opposite to my right. He had just finished changing the scenery and was standing back to observe the play. I could feel my legs shaking underneath my heavy skirts. We were supposed to be busy in the shop as the blackout curtain came up. We were all chattering amongst ourselves and Ann walked on stage from the wings, looking for Arty.

I looked out into the audience and once again noticed Francesca in the audience. '*Don't look, Yabba, what have I said?*' Emily hissed. She was standing behind the till

on stage, watching me. I don't know why I looked out
there again, I just did. *'Help me, Em, where should I stand
now Ann's on stage?'* I felt frozen. I kept saying the word
'philandering' in my head. *'Stop thinking of the line; concentrate on what Ann's saying. Remember you're acting, not just
saying the words. Move over to me near the till. Don't turn your
back to the audience!'* Too late. I swung round to my right
and tried to stay calm. *'You have to look shocked that Ann
doesn't know Arty is with Helen Walsingham.'* I rearranged
my features into my best shocked face. *'That's better, now
participate in the scene; don't think about the cue.'* I think I was
so nervous about the cue because although I *did* know
the words, I had helped Rosie learn them, what I wasn't
so hot on was the song lyrics because Rosie did most
of her singing practice at home. And I don't think even
Emily could disguise the fact that I didn't know the
lyrics very well. *'Don't forget I can tell you the lyrics before you
have to sing them, while Ann's singing. You'll have to concentrate!'*
This was going to be *total* carnage.

I took a deep breath, feeling Jake's gaze on my back,
and got into the swing of the scene, playing my part with
my full attention. Before I knew it, my cue walloped
me in the face. The word, the word—what was it?
Argh! I would say it wrong. 'Not nice—not nice at all!
Phil—' Nooooooooooooo!

'Philandering!' Emily shouted from behind the till. 'Style it out!'

'Philandering.' I made it sound like I was searching for the word and finally remembered it, which was exactly what had happened. And Ann launched into the song 'I Don't Believe a Word of It'. Basically, not wanting to hear what we had to say, which was Arty is two-timing you! I felt my stomach drop down to my little black slip-on shoes. How was I going to pull this off? Emily said, 'Now, we have to sing back at her: "Well, tell us! You're jealous!"' So I did—with Eleanor and Isabella. Thankfully the other two girls were really good singers and loud too, so they could make up for my rubbishness. But the song was long and I couldn't keep up with the pace so I was stuck with no words; I just rhubarbed! I think I was awash with sweat at this point. My white shirt was in danger of becoming see-through on my back. But after a few seconds, I didn't care. I watched Emily's face, smiling happily, singing the words because she could, and I joined in and somehow the song made sense and the words just came to me. It was like all the times before in school plays when we had sung together on stage and we caught each other's eyes and wanted to laugh at the madness of standing in front of hundreds of people singing a show tune. But we loved it. It just felt right.

When I was least expecting it, Eleanor began to drag me to skip around the stage, all the while singing to Ann. I managed to skid in my slip-on shoes. *'I've got you,'* Em said and grabbed my arm to stop me falling flat on my face or possibly tripping and falling forward over the footlights and into the orchestra! Do you know it was exhausting keeping in character, believing that I really was the snidey shop girl Kate, revelling in Ann's heartbreak, at the same time as trying to see where I had to be and what was happening around me? I had folded my face into an Alex Bennett mask to help me concentrate. At the same time my heart was thundering in my ears where I was certain a teeny tiny creature had crawled in with one of those huge bass drums and was banging away like a heavy metal drummer.

When the scene came to a close for us shop girls, I cannot describe the relief. It was like finishing your worst exam, knowing that you've got more exams, but all the other ones you've revised for.

'Well done, Yabba Gabba, you were BRILLIANT!' Emily cooed as we rushed off stage and into the wings. All I could hear was the bass drum in my head. I was so hot, I needed some air. Then I went deaf and my legs went from under me and the wooden floorboards would have come up to greet me with a lovely welcoming thump in

the face, except someone caught me. It was biology all over again except without the cow's eye winking at me.

'Emily?' I whispered aloud. 'I feel funny . . .'

'Put your head between your legs,' a boy's voice said. 'You're making a habit of this . . .'

'Where's Emily?' I said again. I was a bit confused, with my head between my legs in the wings. I felt like I was going to be sick.

'She's not here, Gaby. It's Robbie.' I looked up at him and thought my head was going to explode. Jake was standing next to Robbie who was crouching by me. 'Head back down please.'

Mrs Mooney took over. 'My dear, you did so well. I think you got too hot and stressed. You poor thing. I'll get you some water.' And off she jangled.

'You did really well,' Robbie said. 'Considering you had no idea what you were doing!'

'I wasn't that bad, was I?' I groaned rubbing my temples.

'No, you were really good,' Jake said.

'So why did you want to know where Emily was?' Robbie asked quietly.

I so wasn't expecting him to ask that.

'I didn't, did I?' I wavered, head still down cradled in my knees.

'You did,' he said. 'I heard you.'

'I don't remember saying it.' Which is almost true. It was sort of hazy to me. I just denied it, what could I do, open it up for discussion? Be made to look like a complete and utter nutjob loonbag? As I said before, deny deny deny!

'Well, you did say it.' He wasn't letting it go.

I shrugged. I wasn't getting involved in this. Where was the girl in question anyway?

Luckily, Mrs Mooney came back with the water before it got awkward. 'How are you feeling? Come back here and sit down for a bit, drink this and see how you feel.' She helped me up out of the way of the football team who were getting ready to whip the entire emporium off stage and set the scene for the next part of the story.

I sat on a chair that wasn't being used for a scene and drank out of the squashy white plastic cup. The sub-zero temperature of the water hit my brain like a spade.

'*You OK?*' Emily asked in my head to prevent me talking out loud. She was kneeling beside me. '*Brain freeze?*'

I nodded. The girls were on stage in the chorus, where I should have been, but I don't suppose I would be missed right now.

'*You went white and then keeled over; Robbie grabbed you just before you hit the floor. I didn't want to say anything in case I confused you.*' Emily squeezed my hand. '*He seemed to know what he was doing.*' She looked sad, a bit misty-eyed for a second.

'*I mentioned you and he wouldn't let it lie.*'

'*I know, I heard.*'

'*Why wouldn't he let it lie?*' I asked her. Emily didn't say anything. Then a thought crossed my mind. '*You're not spending time with him as well, are you? When you're not with me?*'

'*No! No one sees me, only you.*' But there was something she wasn't telling me. I'm not her best friend for nothing.

'Gabriella, are you feeling like you want to be in the second act or do you want to sit this one out and leave it?' Mrs Mooney asked, looming over me, clipboard in hand, drumming her talons along the top of it.

Emily looked pleadingly at me. I felt OK now. 'I think the words are: the Show Must Go On!' I said and got up. Emily clapped her hands together in glee.

'What a trouper!' Mrs M said smiling. 'Let's get you changed and ready for the final push.'

AFTERSHOW PARTY SHENANIGANS

The cheering made me feel like someone had just injected me with a shot of feel-goodness. I think I could have stooped to hugging Alexandra Bennett even after a really sly insult directed at my jug ears. The orchestra was playing the finale and it was my turn to take a bow with Eleanor and Isabella. 'Go on girls, you're up,' Andie the stage manager urged, and she gave a little nod for us to walk out on stage. The lights toasted my eyeballs because they were on full whack, but we strode out purposefully, butterflies flapping, hoping not to collide with some scenery, into the middle of the stage and bowed. The audience cheered madly and I looked out, squinting slightly, and spotted Francesca clapping enthusiastically. She noticed that I had clocked her and gave me a thumbs up and nudged her mum and said something to her. Eleanor guided me to the left side of the stage where we awaited everyone else's bows. Jake and Robbie were in the wings opposite, giving me the eagle eye. I felt my tummy flip and with a sinking feeling remembered that I had mentioned Emily when I was having my freak-out.

When Ewan and Matilda came skipping out from opposite wings, meeting centre stage hand in hand looking like love's young dream the audience went ballistic, clapping and cheering then standing up and stamping their feet. We all linked hands and took a team bow. Emily was in front of me and she took a bow too! She turned round to look at me and I laughed at her over-excited bowing. George and Millie were in the same line as me but further down. They both winked at me and we just grinned like loons. I felt so happy; it was just like old times, all of us back together again, doing the same thing, being the fab five that we always were.

'Can I have your attention everyone?' Mrs Mooney was waving around one of those squashy white plastic beakers and I was making a huge assumption that it wasn't full of water.

'Do you think she's drunk?' Millie whispered in my ear, echoing my own thoughts.

'Naaah, she's always like this, isn't she?' I said laughing. We were in the main hall in front of the stage. All the chairs had been cleared away by Mr Preston, the school caretaker. The whole cast, backstage crew, make-up, scenery painters, anyone and everyone involved in the play was there for the aftershow party.

'I just wanted to say how amazing you all are,' Mrs Mooney started off. 'This has been one of the best productions we have ever done in this school . . .'

'She says this every year,' someone said behind me. I craned my neck to see who it was, but the crowd behind me were all looking at her speaking and not saying a thing.

'You have all put one hundred per cent effort into *Half a Sixpence*, from the scenery to the costumes to the front of house to the actors on the stage. You should all be very proud of yourselves and you deserve an enormous standing ovation!'

Ewan Taylor and Matilda Rosen were standing either side of her and started clapping, so we all joined in, some of the boys whooping and cheering as well.

Mrs Mooney bounced her hands, palms down in front of her, to quieten the noise.

'There is someone I want to say a special thank you to. She stepped into Rosie Payne's shoes today at the eleventh hour, and without any rehearsal took on the part of Kate the shop girl. She did an amazing job and deserves a huge round of applause: Gabriella Richards.' And she pointed right at me. I could feel my face flash scarlet and burn like a red hot chilli pepper.

Emily grabbed my hand. *'Good job, Yabba. Look how well you did!'*

'You know I couldn't have done it without you, Em,' I said in my head.

'You would have been great.'

'No, I wouldn't. I can't do any of this without you . . .' She looked at me and was about to say something when Ewan Taylor came over and gave me a big hug and a kiss on the cheek. Oh. My. God!

'Well done, Gaby,' he said in my ear. 'That must have been really hard.' He did indeed smell amazing and I could feel myself go even redder (if that was at all possible; perhaps my hair would start smoking?) and I felt like Rosie must have done when she had to stand next to him in the technical rehearsal for ages. He did have that star quality. He was way above Real Boy status, he was a Man. I could feel the seeds of a crush germinating in my tummy. Oh no. Not a crush. I didn't want one of those. Mooning and staring and being vague like Rosie. But it's almost impossible not to have one when Ewan looks right at you and talks to you! Everyone was cheering, but then I reckon they would have cheered at someone opening an envelope today because we were all on such a high from the end of the play. Emily shouted, 'High five!' super loud and whooped some more for good measure. She was loving the party, even though she couldn't have any pizza.

Then out of nowhere Matilda magicked a large bouquet of super-posh tropical flowers rustling in cellophane and red ribbon and she presented them to Mrs Mooney with a flourish. Mrs Mooney herself went red and bowed dramatically. 'Thank you, my dears,' she cooed. 'Now let's have a party.' One of the lighting boys had plugged an iPod into the sound system on the stage, so we soon had music and we kids had fizzy drinks and mega-topping pizzas, garlic bread and salad, supplied by the kitchen, all laid out on the packed-lunch tables. I think the adults had some fizzy wine as they were getting a bit giggly and Mrs Mooney was getting louder and waving her arms more erratically.

People kept coming up to me and saying how well I had done. Ewan winked at me from across the hall while he was stuffing his face full of pizza and chatting to some of the teachers. I went bright red, *again*!

'What's going on with you?' George asked. 'You're bright red!'

'Ewan just winked at her,' Millie giggled.

'You can't have a crush on him, Rosie does and she will be so cross if you do too! Especially after you took her part for the play.' George was looking stern.

'I *don't* have a crush on him and I didn't take her part—she was ill.' I stuffed the crush to the back of my inner wardrobe. There is a crush hierarchy in our group. If someone has a crush on a Real Boy, no one else is allowed to have the same crush. Or admit to it, anyway! It's just how it has always been. All the way back as far as Infants when Millie and I liked Sam (who's just not as cute any more) and Millie liked him more, so I let her have the crush and I had to make do with having a crush on Bobby (who is not the most handsome boy now to be honest). That's the thing with boys, some of them get hit with the ugly stick as they get older.

'Hey, you were brilliant earlier,' Francesca said as she sidled up to me, pizza perched on paper plate. I hadn't noticed Francesca at the party so far, but knew she must be there. I wondered absently who she had been talking to all this time to have been so elusive. I didn't think she knew anyone apart from me and Robbie and Jake.

'Thanks.'

'How come you knew all the words and stuff?'

'Because I'd helped Rosie learn her lines.'

'Wow, impressive. You really were the part.' She hovered, the others looking at her, interrupting our little group. 'Our scenery looked good, didn't it?'

I smiled. 'It did, yes. We did a good job. Was that your mum you were with?'

'Yes,' she nodded. 'My dad had to sit a few rows back because Mum would have had a meltdown otherwise.' Her face twitched a bit when she said that.

'Oh, that's rubbish,' I said, knowing it must have been hard. I couldn't imagine what it must be like to have parents who can't even be in the same room. I was lucky in that respect, even though Dad worked a lot and quite often wasn't even in the same house!

Someone had turned up the iPod and some dance music blasted out over the stage enticing people to out-do each other's even more ludicrous dance moves. Stragglers started to gravitate towards where we were and gyrate around us like we were a giant handbag at a disco. 'Come on, do you want to dance?' George asked, always one for having a boogie. Millie nodded and followed George into the throng wiggling her hips as she went. Emily ran after them and I wanted to go too. I watched them dancing with Emily, neither of them knowing she was right there with them, grooving like she had done at our birthday party a few months previously. I could feel the pull in my stomach to walk away from Francesca and join my friends, but I knew it was very rude.

'Yes, it was rubbish,' Francesca said quietly. And then suddenly out of nowhere, Robbie and Jake were standing right in our space, hogging the oxygen.

'Can we help you?' Francesca asked, quite coolly. I was very impressed!

'Er, yes, the thing was, is, I was wondering if you two would like to go to the cinema, tomorrow night?' Robbie half stammered out. I had never seen him so wobbly before especially after trying to interrogate me earlier.

'Both of us, with just *you*?' Francesca asked incredulously.

'*Emily! Emily! HELP!*' I shouted in my head. She was there in an instant.

'*What's going down, Yabba?*'

'No, both of us with both of you,' Robbie said awkwardly.

Emily looked on agog. Francesca stared at me, boring her eyes right inside my skull, like she was scanning my brain for an answer or indeed any kind of brain activity as I had somehow turned mute. She looked like she wanted me to make a decision because she was in shock. Just great!

A DOUBLE DATE
CONUNDRUM

'Errrrrm,' Francesca finally managed as my mouth was
still on lockdown.

'*Say yes,*' Emily urged. '*You like Jake, I know you do; you
just won't admit it.*'

'*I don't!*' I squeaked in my head. However, my racing
heart and sweaty palms were telling a different story.

'*You do! You don't know how you feel so that means you like
him!*'

'*But he doesn't even like me; he's been ignoring me since
Rosie's party.*'

'*Why's he asking you out?*'

'*He isn't. Robbie is. And he's asking so he can go with Francesca! Jake's his wing man, I'm the gooseberry.*' That shut her up.

'Girls? One of you going to answer? The film is the latest James Bond if that sways you.' I did love a James Bond film.

Francesca was looking at me with eyes wide. I nodded ever so slightly at her, so slight that you would almost have to be a hawk to have noticed the minuscule movement of my neck. Francesca is obviously a bird of prey then. She turned to the boys. 'We will come with you, but only because it's a James Bond film.'

I don't know why I nodded. Maybe it was the James Bond film clincher. Or perhaps I did really like Jake after all. Maybe he had really asked me out via Robbie like Em suggested. And when that thought registered, my tummy flipped in excitement . . . Emily was going to be very smug about this revelation now.

'Outside the cinema at eight tomorrow night then?' Robbie asked, back to his normal confident self, and he and Jake wandered off to get more pizza. Jake looked over his shoulder at me.

Emily was very quiet. I looked at her, but before I could say anything (sorry for saying that about Robbie perhaps?) the girls ran over.

'What happened there?' George asked, keen to get the goss.

'Robbie asked Gaby and me out to the cinema,' Francesca said.

'What?! Both of you with just *him*?' Millie gasped.

'No, with Jake as well,' I replied sighing.

'That's a bit weird,' George said.

'Is it?' I asked, sort of realizing it but felt I had to ask anyway just to check.

'It just is. Think about it,' she glared at me, not unkindly. More in an 'it's obvious and you should realize' way.

'Oh, yeah, I suppose,' I said, getting it for real.

Francesca just looked on and stood there, not moving.

'Why is it weird?' Millie asked the question again, being a bit dim. 'It's obvious Jake likes Yabba and that's why they're going out, isn't it? You guys are having secrets!'

'We're not, believe me,' George said. 'I'll tell you when we go and get more pizza. Come on. You want anything, girls?' We both shook our heads, I still hadn't made a dent in my plate of food.

'What's going on?' Francesca asked as soon as they ambled off to fill their faces. 'And why do they call you Yabba?'

Emily had been very quiet in all of this. I felt odd having the conversation with Francesca knowing Emily was there, listening. It didn't seem right. For the first time ever, I needed to be . . . *on my own.* It was a hard thing to realize and not something I ever thought would happen. And I knew Emily would hear it and I didn't want to think it.

'*I'm going to see what George and Millie are up to,*' Emily said breezily, shooting me a megawatt smile and a secret wink. '*I can look at the pizza and pretend I can eat it.*' I smiled gratefully at her and watched her glide through the bobbing heads.

'Yabba Gabba is . . . *was* Emily's nickname for me. It just stuck in our group.' Everyone was going a teensy bit bananas all around us now as the iPod shuffled to a chart favourite. Even some of the teachers were getting up and making idiots of themselves. Surely they would regret it on Monday? I felt like we were in an advert on the telly where everyone else knew the moves to a public rave and we were completely out of the loop wondering what on earth all the fuss was about.

'Shall we move over there?' Francesca suggested and we picked our way through the mass of arms flailing around and hitting us in the face like missiles. We headed back towards the stack of chairs at the side of the hall, near the gargantuan over-decorated Christmas tree. The comforting woodland smell of pine needles and fairy-light-frazzled tinsel filled my nostrils and conjured up dreams of Santa and enticingly wrapped presents. I craned my neck to see where George and Millie were. I couldn't spot Emily with them. But some tall guy suddenly moved and I could just see her, standing by the last of the pizza slices, eyeing them up like a praying mantis.

'The reason George said it's weird that we are going out with Robbie is that if this situation had happened a few months ago, Emily would be going to the cinema with Robbie. It would be Robbie and Emily.'

'Oh. So Emily and Robbie were girlfriend and boyfriend?'

'Pretty much, if you *can* be girlfriend and boyfriend *without* being girlfriend and boyfriend.'

'So they weren't? I'm confused.'

'Robbie really liked Emily, everyone knew that. We have all known each other since infant school. But no one really did girlfriend, boyfriend stuff at primary school. Not properly. Not unless you were Alexandra Bennett. She would be going out with someone at university if she could! We just hung out. But Robbie and Emily hung out a lot.' Francesca looked disappointed.

'What about you and Jake?' she eventually asked after I had wolfed down some pizza to fill the awkward gap that revelation created.

'Errr . . . nothing really. You know he's Robbie's best friend, his wing man.'

'But he likes you, doesn't he?'

'I don't know.'

'A blind man could spot it, Gaby. You accidentally dissed him at Rosie's party. I reckon he's too scared to ask you himself so he's got Robbie to ask you out for him.' That's just what Emily had said. Half of me wanted this to be true, but then I remembered all the nutjobby things I've said to him regarding Emily. He must think I'm mental. Were boys *this* bothered about girls? I had no idea, not my usual territory. I only knew how we were—giggly and silly, not really expecting anything to *ever* happen. Now it was, it was a whole new ball game. 'This is about you and Jake, not about me and Robbie. I could be anyone.'

'If that's the case then why didn't he ask Millie or George?' I said.

Francesca shrugged. 'I don't know. We won't find out unless we ask them, right now.' She was a mad one, that's for sure! Maybe going to an all girls' school makes you slightly loopy and able to always ask in-your-face questions—she had a habit of it.

'We can't ask them!'

'Why not?'

'No one does things like that!' Not even Emily when she wasn't dead.

'Oh . . . Looks like we're going on a date then.' And she laughed nervously. I started to wonder what I was going to wear. Would I wear dark skinny Mango jeans or my denim mini? Very very under the radar I began to feel the buzz of anticipation about our date with the boys.

'Do you actually *like* Robbie then?' I asked, curious to see what she would say. So she had never liked Jake at all then. It was Robbie all along.

'Who wouldn't? He's cute, isn't he?' she said way too casually, *almost* like she didn't care. She was trying to be cool about it, as cool as an ice cube on a sightseeing holiday at the North Pole, but she wasn't fooling me. I had seen her go red sometimes when he talked to her. I was pretty confident she liked him, but would never let on, now she knew about Emily . . .

So . . . we were going on a double date, no triple date, but only I knew that.

'Yabba, no way am I coming with you. It wouldn't be right.' We were in my room and I was getting my purple and white spotty shorts and vest top on for bed.

'But I can't go without you. I can't,' I said sulkily. My psychic ability had told me this conversation was going to nosedive. I should have my own psychic hotline I was so accurate! Gypsy Rose Gaby.

'Think about it, Gaby, I would be the gooseberry.' Emily was sitting on my bed, fiddling with her hair, something she had always done when she was thinking about something she would rather not think about. Mostly Maths tests if I remember rightly.

'You wouldn't! You're not even slightly green or hairy!' She laughed at my pathetic stab at humour. 'Only I'd know you were there, no one else.' I really couldn't see a way of getting her to come. 'You could bring a date with you!'

'Oh, yeah, great. Elvis again?' she snapped back.

'I *knew* you were holding out on Elvis!'

'Everything all right, Gaby?' Mum asked from the other side of the door. She and Dad were going to bed. We had got back from the party quite late. George's mum had picked us up.

'Fine, Mum,' I replied, wincing at getting caught talking to Emily out loud again.

'Night, lovely.'

I pressed my ear to the crack in the door to hear them go into their room.

'What was wrong with Gaby?' I heard Dad ask.

'The usual,' Mum replied. 'Talking to herself again, but I don't like it. It's not normal. She was talking about Elvis.' The door shut and all I could hear was *rhubarb rhubarb*.

I turned round and Emily looked at me squarely, continuing the conversation in our heads. '*I think we need to try this date with you going on your own.*' My stomach sank to the bottom of my orange sparkly toenails. Gypsy Rose Gaby was right. '*There'll be no point me being there. You're on a date! With Jake, who really likes you. And Robbie, who's going with Francesca. It's too . . . weird.*' She was right. I knew that, I just didn't *want* to know it.

'*I won't go then,*' I sighed, surprisingly disappointed that I wouldn't be going at all.

'*Come on, it will be fun,*' she chided. '*You like Jake, admit it.*'

I couldn't own up she was right for once. Something was stopping me from being entirely honest. But I didn't need to be, Emily could read me like a book.

'*The first time doing things without me is going to be hard. But it has to start sometime.*'

'*Why?*' I asked feeling a flip of fear in my tummy that had jumped in a lift and returned to its rightful place.

'*Did you think I was going to stay here for ever?*'

'*Yes! Why wouldn't you?*'

'*Because there's a whole world out there, waiting for Gaby Richards to be in it.*'

'*I* am *in it.*'

'*You're not, Yabba,*' she said softly. '*You are when you feel safe with me.*'

'*So I am in it!*'

'*But what happens when I'm not there.*'

I went quiet. I couldn't think about the world when Emily wasn't in it. It was just too hard, and sad, and stomach-churningly awful, that I hadn't had to think about it for months, properly.

'*So will you go on the date?*' The black hole of tomorrow loomed up to greet me and I didn't know the answer.

TO GO OR NOT TO GO

I lay in bed, getting eaten alive by the duvet as it trapped my limbs in its clutches, twisting me this way and that. *To go or not to go*, that is the question. Emily had disappeared, I was alone with my thoughts, or was I? I never knew if she was here or not when she said she wasn't. She only left just before I fell asleep usually, but I couldn't sleep. I didn't even want a Malteser from my secret stash to help me on my way. I hadn't even asked Mum if it was OK for me to go as I didn't want her to say yes. She would say yes too because she was desperate for me to go out and be with people instead of being a total nutjob talking to myself.

The thought of not going with Emily was . . . how was it? Unthinkable? Not really. I had managed the scenery painting totally fine. But this was a whole date, an *actual date*, with a boy. And not just any boy; Jake, whom I (and let's be honest here) like properly. But since Em . . . died, I sort of went off him temporarily. And I wasn't on the date with George or Millie, but *Francesca*. She wasn't my other half. She didn't finish my sentences for me. She didn't know what was in my head (a very small brain and a mini Dime bar). She didn't know me and she wasn't Emily.

The duvet gnawed on my leg and I kicked if off and lay in the dark sighing. Maybe a Malteser would help. I reached under the bed and teased the old shoe box out and grabbed a pack, crunching one in my mouth immediately. Yuck yuck yuck. It tasted like warm sugary milk. Gross. I shouldn't have had one. Where were the Dime bars?

I woke with a start, daylight streaming through a sliver of uncovered window. My right eye felt like it was a poached egg. Emily was sitting on the chair to my dressing table looking at me. 'You sleep OK?' she said, smoothing down her angelic-looking glossy mane of hair.

'No, awful. I kept waking up.'

'Guilty conscience?'

'No!!! I just couldn't sleep.'

'So, are you going to the cinema?'

I shrugged. Even all the tossing and turning and thinking and rethinking hadn't made it any clearer.

'Think of it like this: you like James Bond. You like Robbie and you like Jake. You might like Francesca if you thought about it. See what happens. You might have a nice time.'

'I would go if you would be there.'

'I can't, you know that.'

'Then that's my answer.' I knew I was cutting off my nose to spite my face, but I just couldn't imagine Emily not being there. I would rather stay in with her here.

As the clock crept round to six o'clock I felt sicker and sicker. I knew I had to give the guys notice that I wasn't going to go. I had had a million texts from the girls all wishing me luck, hoping I had a nice time, asking what I was wearing, etc., etc. I even got one from Rosie who wanted to hear all about the play.

'You need to ring Robbie,' Emily said calmly. Emily had given me his number to ring. 'You need to tell him so they can decide what to do. And you need to tell

Francesca.' I didn't have her number. 'I've got it here, put it in your phone.' And I punched it in into my contacts with a bit of a wavering hand.

'Gaby, can I have a word?' Mum knocked at my door just as I was about to dial. Saved by the bell. 'We're going to decorate the Christmas tree in a mo, do you want to come down and help?' We had all been out as a family earlier that day to choose the tree from outside the Dog and Duck pub down in the town. It was tradition as far back as I can remember that we all went. Mum would ummm and ahhhhh thoughtfully, asking to see all different ones, pulling on the arms of the trees checking for needle droppage and how it hung. I always wanted a really small one and Mum always wanted one that would have filled Leicester Square. We got one that spread its branches wide in the living-room bay window, its green fingers touching opposite sides of the window frame, the smell scenting the room with magic and promises of surprises and sparkle and fun.

Mum poked her head round the door. Emily looked up at her and I, always fearful she would spot her, did a double take to make sure she couldn't see her.

'What's going on? You look like you're up to something.'

'No, I was just about to ring someone.'

'Anyone I know?' She sounded all eager and keen to find out.

'No, just a girl from school.'

'Someone new? Why don't you invite her round?'

I looked at her like she was mad. 'Mum, I'm just ringing her about something else. I'm not about to invite her round. We're doing the tree anyway.'

'I didn't mean now, I meant after school one day.' She went quiet for a moment and I knew what was coming . . .

'Your dad and I are worried about you.' She came into the room properly now and stood with her back to the half-open door. 'You spend too much time on your own. I know you sometimes see George, Rosie, and Millie, but a lot of the time you're either up here or watching TV by yourself. Before Emily died you guys were always up to so much, as a group.'

'I'm fine, Mum, honestly, I really am. I just want to be on my own sometimes. And I do things with the girls. I went to the sleepover.'

'Yes, and came back bald,' she retorted. I sometimes forget I've got no hair any more and my ears do get cold! Probably because they stick out so much.

'I did the play as well, I painted the scenery and I was in it by accident!' I wasn't a freak. No one else thought so, apart from maybe Robbie and Jake.

'Yes, love, I know. Sorry.' She did look like maybe I had convinced her. I didn't think I was too much of a hermit. I had been out quite a few times, but she was right, I didn't invite people here. 'Look, after Christmas maybe try and get out more. To the cinema or something. Invite the girls back for tea after school—we never see them any more! A new year, a fresh start and all that. Your dad and I are talking about taking a holiday at half term next year, somewhere hot. So that will be a great thing to do, something to look forward to. Maybe you could bring along George, Millie, or Rosie too?'

I nodded, smiling dumbly. I was sure I could get out of bringing someone. And I couldn't pick just one of them; that would be wrong. It's either all of them or none of them. They come as a package of three, just like Emily and I came as a package of two. I wanted to spend my hot holiday with Emily, lounging on the beach, laughing at our stupid in-jokes.

'I'll come down in a sec to decorate the tree, OK?' She nodded and left the room.

'You heard what your mum said, go out more! Go to the cinema!'

'But I really, really don't want to go.'

'Then phone the guys and let them know.' She crossed her arms and waited while I summoned up the courage to do so. She wasn't being haughty or cross, but I could tell she wasn't impressed. I don't think I was impressed with myself either, but I couldn't help how I felt, could I?

'You *can* help how you feel, everyone can. You're just choosing to not want to go,' Emily said sagely.

'But what if I have an awful time? What if I don't know what to say and you're not there to help me.'

Emily laughed. 'You not knowing what to say is like saying you will win the Nobel Prize for Maths. Total rubbish! You can talk for England!'

'But . . .'

'But nothing. I think the question should be: what if you have a great time? I think that's what scares you!'

I opened my mouth to say something, but nothing came out. I didn't like arguing with Emily, so I didn't. She's just so wise now, it's very confusing! I rang Robbie instead.

'Hi, Robbie, it's Gaby,' I said, trying not to sound too relieved.

'Hey, let me guess, you're not coming tonight.'

'How did you know?'

'Just a wild guess. You've had all day to come up with an excuse, so let's hear it.' Mind blank, help. Argh! I pulled a 'please help me' face at Emily, but she was reading a magazine and not looking at me. I had to go it alone.

'Well, Mum said I couldn't go. We're busy this evening, last minute plans I didn't know about until just now.' Yep, decorating that tree was über important!

'Whatever, Gaby. Thanks for letting me know. I'll be sure to tell Jake.' Ouch. That was harsh. One down, two to go.

'Hello, Francesca? It's Gaby.'

'Oh, hi. How did you get this number?'

'Er . . . I thought you gave it to me?' Lie lie lie!

'I can't remember. Maybe I did. Are you all set for tonight? What are you wearing?' She sounded so excited. I suddenly felt really really bad. Saying it to Robbie was OK, but to Francesca, I felt like a toad.

'That's the thing.'

'The thing?' She suddenly changed tone and sounded like someone who was just about to be massively let down.

'Mum said I can't go.'

'Oh no! Why?'

'Because I didn't realize we were going out already, she only just told me and I have to go.' My excuse was as lame as a blind beggar with one leg hobbling along a potholed road.

'Never mind. I guess you have to go if your mum says so.'

'Yeah. What will you do?' Why oh why did I ask that one?

'Well, I'm not going without you, am I? I guess I'll watch *X Factor*.' It was on the tip of my tongue to say the same, when I remembered I was lying about going out, so I zipped my lip.

'I'm really sorry,' I said limply, now feeling like a germ living on the back of the smallest atom in the world, inside the squelchy nostril of a giant toad.

'It's OK. Don't worry about it. I hope you have a nice evening. See you on Monday.' Why did she always, always have to be so nice? It was so thoughtless of her to make ignoring her so flipping hard! You can't be horrid to nice, can you? Grrr . . .

'So, all done?' Emily asked, pretending she hadn't just heard me on the phone.

'Yep.'

'You must feel relieved to have got it out of the way.'

'Nope, I feel worse now.'

She gave me a wiser than wise smile like Yoda and sucked in her lips. 'It's done now and it's how we learn. Move on from it, don't spoil your evening. We're going to decorate the tree now. Come on.'

How did she get to be so clever? And what was I going to learn?

'Elvis taught me well, don't you think?' she laughed and pushed me out of the door so we could go mad with the tinsel.

THE BEST OF DAYS,
THE WORST OF DAYS

She wasn't there. I rubbed my eyes; no, I wasn't imagining it, she just wasn't there. I sat up in bed and stretched. Maybe she had gone to the loo. Doughnut—angels don't go to the loo. '*Emily?*' I said in my head, careful not to alarm anyone who happened to be ear-wigging at my door. Silence. '*Em?*' I didn't understand. She had never not been there when I woke up before. Maybe there had been an Elvis emergency and she'd had to go on a course or something? Learn how to do miracles and stuff like that.

I thought back to yesterday, Sunday, and maybe she had told me she wasn't going to be here today. We'd had such a great weekend. On Saturday night we had all decorated the tree. She had laughed and joked with me in my head as me and Max put all the decorations on the tree in a higgledy-piggledy manner, only for Mum to come along five minutes later and rearrange it all so it looked more even and perfect, her idea of how a beautifully styled tree should look on the magazine shoot blazing away in her head.

Then Mum cooked the most amazing spicy sticky chicken with crispy roast potatoes and a chocolate fudge cake for afters. Max and I had to stir the mincemeat she made too and make a Christmas wish. We all sat down to watch *X Factor*, me hiding behind a cushion as the boy band that I liked sang totally out of tune and ruined their chances of winning, Emily squealing when her favourite act got a good feedback from all the judges, Mum rolling her eyes and pretending not to watch, but keeping getting sucked in. I asked Em who was going to win, but she said she didn't know. I bet she did!

Then on Sunday Mum and Dad took us ice skating. There was a sparkly perfectly triangular Christmas tree towering statuesquely over the centre of the rink that was outside in the park on the other side of town. It was a once-a-year spectacular and we had all gone last year with Emily and her family. Me and Em had spent the whole time falling over and giggling and not really leaving the side while our mums went for it like total loons.

But this time Emily glided round the rink in a pure-white skating outfit: white boots, white woolly tights, short white fur-trimmed skating skirt and matching jacket with pom-poms, and a white woolly hat. All that was missing was her angel wings. I was in jeans and my parka because it was freezing. '*How come you can ice skate all of a sudden like a pro in that outfit?*' I asked, clinging on to the side, wanting to let go but not quite trusting. Mum was whizzing round with Max, and Dad was sort of OK, but kept tripping, ramming into crowds of people and clinging to the sides for balance.

'*I haven't got the fear any more because I can't hurt myself, can I?*' That made sense. But I could hurt myself, easily. Mum had offered to take me round, but I'd said I wanted to acclimatize first. Emily didn't mention where her professional ice-skating outfit had materialized from; another angelic secret I guess. '*Take my hand, I'll take you round.*' Emily beckoned with her right hand, trying to tempt me from the safety of the wooden sides. 'It's easy once you have a go, trust me . . .'

So I let go and she grabbed my left hand and guided me round the outside of the rink. My other arm was held right out to balance me. I stumbled a few times but

Em tightened her grip on my hand and wouldn't let me fall over.

'*You're doing really well. We've been round twice now, let's pick up the pace.*' I nodded, trying to concentrate on the ice in front, who was where, how far from the edge I was, was someone going to crash into me, would I break a leg . . .

'Wow, Gaby, you're up and away!' Mum shouted at me as she skated past holding Max's hand. 'Do you want Dad to help?' Wasn't that like asking a blind man to help a decrepit old lady cross the road?

'I think I will just try on my own, ta.'

Mum zoomed off. 'Faster!' Em cried aloud, laughing at my face. 'Don't think about the disasters that could happen, think about how free you feel and how fast you can go. Come on!'

Her arm yanked mine and my legs followed, one in front of the other, stiffly at first, but then more smoothly, until I was in step with Emily. I was skating! I wasn't worrying about people crashing into me or me crashing into anyone else, I was just skating. 'It's fun, isn't it?' Emily cried above the cheesy Christmas music blaring out of the speakers and bouncing off all the skaters.

'Yes!' I cried out loud, not caring if anyone heard me. It was exhilarating!

I lost myself in the rhythm of the skating, whizzing round and round, weaving in and out of people, my legs burning. I passed a girl that looked just like Emily in the pom-pom outfit. It was Emily! *'You let go!'* I tried shouting in my head.

'Yes I did, but look, you can skate! All by yourself, properly.'

'I know, but I didn't feel you let go.' I had slowed down and was skating by her side.

'You didn't need me any more; you weren't leaning on me so I let you go. And you whizzed off like a bullet from a gun!'

'What next?' I asked.

'Let's try to skate backwards!' Emily laughed and skated off in front of me, beckoning me to follow.

That evening at home, after I had done my homework, we chilled in my room, listening to my iPod.

'Yabba, I've had a really great weekend with you. It was just like old times. I'll remember this weekend for ever as being one of the best.'

'Me too,' I said. 'Learning to skate was amaiiiizing and I want to go again soon.'

'Yes, you should. Go with the girls, I think they'd like that.'

As I lay down under the duvet and drifted off to sleep, I felt a kiss on my forehead. 'Sweet dreams, Yabba,' Emily whispered. 'I miss you already. And remember, I'm always safe and sound as a pound when I'm not with you . . .'

'See you tomorrow,' I slurred like a drunk person before dropping into the black zone of restful sleep.

And here we are: no Emily to report. I looked under the bed, inside the wardrobe, behind the curtains. Deep breath, she will turn up. She always has before. I got dressed. A long white feather fell out of my school jumper as I pulled it on over my head. I snatched it up and smelt it—chocolate. It was from Emily. She was probably busy somewhere else and just wanted me to know she was on her way.

'Are you OK, Gaby?' Mum asked at breakfast as I pushed my waffle round my plate trying to hide it under my sliced banana. Of course that wasn't going to work—a waffle is far too hefty, brown, crunchy and covered in maple syrup to even think for one minute that it could disguise itself as a more delicate morsel like banana. Dream on, waffle . . .

'Yep, fine.'

'You don't look it. It's almost the end of term, I thought you would be excited.'

'Mmmmm,' was all I could muster up. Dog wrapped herself round my ankles, sensing that all was not OK in my world.

The bus wasn't much better. The girls wanted to know why I hadn't gone on the date.

'I just didn't want to go,' I said listlessly.

'But why?' Rosie insisted, back to full wellness after the vomit bug from hell.

'Because I didn't.'

'Well, what did you do instead?' Millie asked all interested.

'I watched *X Factor* and decorated the Christmas tree.'

'Are you OK, Yabba? You don't seem yourself,' George enquired looking concerned.

My eyes filled with tears and I furiously blinked them away. Why was I crying? What was *wrong* with me? I stared out of the window and swallowed down the fear creeping like a thief up my throat. 'I'm OK, I think I'm just coming down with something.'

'Oh God, I hope it's not that sick bug I had,' Rosie gasped. 'It was like dying . . .' And she regaled our group with her deathbed scenario once more, embellishing parts. 'And there really was another person in the toilet with me when Gaby went to get Mrs Mooney. I could feel them there.'

'Did you see them?' Millie asked, agog.

'Not exactly, but I dunno, they were just there.'

'Maybe it was your guardian angel,' George scoffed.

'It could have been,' Rosie agreed, not realizing George was joking.

The bus stopped and Francesca got on. She looked at me and waved and then sat down at the front where she always sat.

'I wonder if she went on the date?' Millie asked. 'Did she?' she asked me.

'I don't think so, but who knows?' I did wonder too, but finding out would mean asking and having to talk to her, and I didn't want to. Then Robbie and Jake got on and even amid my own panic and worry regarding Emily's whereabouts, I dreaded seeing them.

'Uh-oh,' Rosie whistled under her breath. 'Look out!'

Robbie looked over and gave me a steely glare. I just looked away, out of the window, and asked Emily to come quickly.

'If you had been made of ice then, he would have melted you with that glare!' George said quietly. I shrugged. Right now the only thing that mattered was Emily reappearing any time soon. Something tickled my palm. There was a white feather on my lap. I secreted it in my bag and felt slight relief that it was going to be OK. She was just held up.

Francesca sat down next to me in form room. Right now, I don't think I could face niceness, enquiries about my weekend, any chat of any description at all. 'Are you all right, Gaby?' was all she said. I must have looked a bit all at sea.

'Fine, just coming down with something.'

'Maybe you should go home?' I shook my head. Home was worse, it was so quiet. She let me be, but kept looking at me sideways. The morning's lessons dragged on and on like a slow torturous dentist visit without any kind of pain relief.

'Emily? Are you there? Em? Em?' This was my mantra for the whole morning. I couldn't concentrate. I had to read out loud in English and I kept tripping over the story, not being able to pronounce long words because my tongue felt too big for my mouth. Just when I thought I would go mad, I felt a feather tickling my leg and looked down under the desk to see one stuck to my woolly tights. My slouch bag would be a slouch pillow before long. I breathed another sigh of relief and calmed down. *'It'll be OK, it'll be OK, it'll be OK,'* became my new mantra.

'Who's coming for lunch?' Rosie asked at the end of Physics. 'Yabba? You reckon a lamb hotpot could cheer you up?'

'I think it might,' I said, hoping it would, but not feeling even remotely interested in food. There was a faint rumble in my tummy, but not the usual roar of starvation hunger pangs chomping at the bit and rattling their cages.

ROBBIE SPILLS HIS GUTS

The dinner queue snaked out of the canteen and down the corridor. Everyone must have been starving at the same time and not willing to wait one second. 'My stomach thinks my throat has been cut,' Rosie complained as she surveyed the busy scene. 'Queue barging? Anyone up for it?' She would have as well if one of us agreed.

I was standing behind the girls, whispering in my head: '*It will be OK, it will be OK, it will be OK.*' As we shuffled along, up the stairs and into the canteen, the girls chatted excitedly about Christmas and what they hoped to be getting.

'I really really hope I get those ankle boots I want,' Millie sighed. 'They are so so cool; you can wear them

with little dresses or leggings and jeans.' And then she described them in detail—the same ones George wanted too. Rosie wanted a military-style jacket. 'What do you want, Gaby?' George asked me.

I had to stop myself from saying 'my best friend', but that's what I did want, nothing else at all. I made myself say, 'New boots, my old ones are squashed to death.' Who cares about Christmas? I wanted to scream.

'Hey, Gaby, how you doing?' Ewan Taylor said as he breezed past me with his empty lunch tray, dumping it on the tray trolley. 'Did you have a good weekend?' He gave me a dazzling smile as well, almost toothpaste advert standard.

Through the fog I noticed him and smiled. 'Yes thanks, and you?' I *must* be coming down with something, I didn't even get a stomach flip.

'Great thanks. Went to a party. You have a good day. Bye, ladies . . .' The others said 'bye' with fluttering eyelashes.

'Gaby! Oh. My. God! What's wrong with you, he was being nice and you were just too cool for school!' Rosie was almost choking. 'He didn't even remember my name!' She looked devastated.

'Sorry, Rosie. I just don't feel great. I didn't *ask* him to come up and say hello.'

'I think even if I had been at death's door I would have managed more enthusiasm than what you just dredged up.'

'Don't mind her,' George teased, 'she's just jealous her boyfriend prefers you!' Rosie punched her in the arm. 'Ow! My, my, the green-eyed monster is strong in this one . . .'

'I saw him first,' Rosie sulked.

'He's all yours,' I said. 'Knock yourself out.' My minicrush on Ewan fully extinguished.

'Hey, look, we're here,' Millie exclaimed excitedly as we approached the dishes of food on offer today. 'No lamb hotpot though, Yabba. Sorry!' I shrugged. It was no surprise to me, today wasn't exactly in my top ten.

Food hunted and gathered, we had to find a place to sit. The canteen was heaving and there were no places to sit together. 'Let's split up and sit anywhere; if places become free, we'll grab them,' George commanded in her best Operation Canteen voice. The others found spots. I couldn't see anywhere. I waited, steam rising off my tray of beans, cheese, and jacket potato. Someone stood up but as I weaved my way through the sea of moulded plastic chairs I noticed that the free place was opposite Francesca. I started to back away. I just didn't want to sit there. She hadn't noticed me because she was talking to Ellie. I crept backwards, but there was a chair or something in the way. I looked round. Nothing was there. I tried to move back again but couldn't. I was being blocked *'Emily?'* I said in my head. *'Is that you?'* No answer, but I knew it was her, who else would it be? I stepped forward, that worked; backwards, resistance. *'I know what you're doing and it's not going to work,'* I said in my head again. *'I'm not sitting with Francesca.'* But try as I might I couldn't get through and the only way was to walk past Francesca and she would surely see me. I stood where I was, shaking. No one else was moving and people were starting to notice me standing there, looking like a right odd bod. Robbie glanced up from his tray of food piled high and caught my eye. I turned away. I didn't need any grief from him right now.

'Just try it, just sit there, see what happens,' Emily whispered.

'No!' I cried out loud. People did look properly now and I only had one choice, to sit down. I felt sweaty; trickles of moisture started beading under my armpits. I wished I could jump into a hole and be swallowed up right here in the canteen like some hotshot sci-fi movie. The walls were closing in on me giving me the spins, people were staring and someone was laughing. Argh! I stumbled to the place opposite Francesca and slammed my tray down, making her jump and anyone else who hadn't noticed my slide into insanity turn round and stare. I was angry at her for wanting to be friends, angry at Emily for making me feel like this. And as I slammed the tray down, I saw a white feather lying in the centre of the plastic dinner chair. Francesca looked so alarmed.

'Gaby? What's wrong?' she asked. Ellie was looking at me like I might have just tunnelled out of Lunatics 'R' Us. Where were the doctors? Tranquillizer gun needed urgently! Nurse!

George stood up from her seat over the other side and craned her neck to see what was going on.

'Nothing,' I growled, tears now pricking my eyes. And I walked away, squeezing past people's chairs. Half running to the door so I could get out. I saw Robbie jump up and head over to Francesca and then I legged it out of the door, George shouting after me to wait.

I didn't know where I was going to go. I just ran. I sped out of the back entrance by the canteen and ran into the biting cold December air, with its promise of snow lingering in the low grey clouds above. I didn't have a coat; it was on my peg in the form room. Tears were now blinding me. Luckily not many people were about because it was lunchtime and they were all safely ensconced inside hiding from Jack Frost. As I ran down the main path at the back of the school, I realized I was running to the gate, to leave the premises. My bag with house keys, phone, money were all back at school, but I couldn't go back there. So I just kept on running. I could have run a marathon I was so full of energy. My legs felt as light as feathers and I had enough breath to fill my lungs without gasping at all. Why couldn't I summon up this athletic prowess when it mattered? Like on sports day? I could have run everyone into the ground!

As I neared the gate, I heard someone shouting my name. I turned round, it was Robbie. I wanted to punch the release button on the gate, but stopped. He caught up with me, his football fitness coming in handy. 'Where are you off to?' he asked, not too out of breath.

I shrugged. Too scared to speak, terrified what might come out of my mouth.

'I saw the feather on your seat. Is that why you ran off?' I didn't say a word, just looked wordlessly at him. My nose started to run and I wiped it away with the cuff of my cardigan. The cold seeped into my bones now I had stopped running and I started to shake.

'Look, come inside, you're shaking.'

'No!' I practically shouted.

'Easy, tiger . . . I get those feathers too.'

'What? Really?'

'Yes, really. I have been getting them for months. Since Emily . . . you know.'

'Does anyone else know?'

'What do you think?' I nodded. It was insane even having this conversation. 'They freaked the life out of me at first, but when that one in the canteen floated down from the ceiling, and I saw that you were totally freaked by it too, it didn't make me feel so mad. I didn't know whether that was for me or you and I couldn't ask you.'

'It was for me. I was having a bad day.'

'Look, don't tell anyone about them,' he said. 'I can't have the guys thinking I'm mental, like you. I had to, you know, cover it up a bit in front of Jake and Francesca.'

'What do you mean, like me? I'm not mental.' This was taking a turn for the worst.

'Jake told me what you said in the broom cupboard, and when you fainted, you asked where Emily was, like you're still hanging out . . . or something.'

What to say to that? I remained quiet for a moment and then said: 'I don't see her, I just *want* to see her, so badly . . .' Tears sprang from my eyes and welled over my lashes and trickled down my cheeks, freezing on my face. And it was true, I hadn't seen her since yesterday, the longest absence since she had come back. I knew she was there like she was in the canteen a minute ago. She was testing me. 'I can do stuff if I *imagine* she's there . . . '

'Ah. I get that. When I started getting the feathers, it took me a while to realize they were probably, you know, from . . . her.' He looked totally squirmy saying that. It was such an unboylike subject to have to talk about. 'But getting them really helped. When she died it was . . . hideous.' He jammed his fists into his trouser pockets and kicked a stone off into the bushes, obviously finding it hard even thinking about it.

'Where do you keep the feathers?' I asked wiping the tears away with my sleeve.

'Under my bed in a plastic bag. I don't know what to do with them! Throwing them away would be . . . wrong.'

'Mine are in an empty pillow case and it's almost full.'

We stood there, both of us taking in the new information we had about each other. I understood why I felt Em was holding out on me about Robbie. She was messaging him too.

'So why did you blow us out on Saturday?' Oh no . . .

'I didn't want to come after all.'

'He's going to kill me for saying this, but Jake really likes you.'

'Oh. *Why*, if I'm so mental?'

'You'd know that everyone likes you, Gaby, if you actually bothered to notice,' he said really quietly. 'When you got your hair cut, well, you sort of became . . . Miss Popular.' Francesca wasn't lying then. I hadn't believed her when she'd mentioned it. Normally I would have been so excited by such unexpected news, but everything was just so rubbish that it hardly registered.

'I don't want a boyfriend,' I said half-heartedly, repeating the mantra I had flung back at Emily every time she had mentioned Jake. But then suddenly, out of nowhere, came the feeling that I may just have messed up.

'You don't say. I think Jake's got the message now.'

Robbie had just told me for certain that Jake liked me, madness and all. And I was screwing it up for real now. Did I really not want a boyfriend? I don't know what I wanted any more. I was too scared to properly find out. I knew I wanted Emily to come and help me sort out my head. It was all spilling about in there and not making any sense. None of it did. I needed a wing woman, someone to talk to.

'You really don't like him then?' he asked.

'I've got to go,' I said quickly. The shakes were overtaking me, the cold penetrating deep down now.

'Where?'

'I've no idea, but I'm not staying here. I can't think and school isn't helping.'

'What do I tell Jake?'

'I don't know, Robbie.'

'You can't just run away, Gaby.'

'Watch me.' I banged my fist on the release button, the gate clicked and I pushed through it, leaving Robbie staring at me as I sprinted off.

FaCiNG tHe TRUTH
WiTH MaRiSa

Out I slipped, into the real world where people worked and lived and breathed normal lives without angels coming along and ruining it all. I took off in the direction of home, but knowing I wasn't going there, not sure where I was going. It was about two kilometres, so not far, but to my unaccustomed distance legs, surely it would feel like a marathon after all.

I only stopped once when I couldn't get across the main road in one go; there was too much traffic and I didn't fancy joining Emily just yet. The only part of me that was cold was my hands after the exercise had warmed me up. They were almost blue at the fingertips. I blew on them while I waited for a gap in the traffic. But I needed proper warmth, a roaring fire or a burning radiator. I spotted a gap in the cars and ran across the road and carried on up the hill, past the first lot of shops on the high street. I was jogging now, my legs weary, the fight squeezed out of me. I was proper tired and I ground to a halt in front of a shop. It was The Brown Bag, the shop that Emily's mum, Marisa, owned. It had a really cool display of glittery tops all spilling out of Santa's sleigh and arranged creatively on the fake-snow-covered rooftop with a chimney and a stuffed pigeon! Santa was nowhere to be seen; maybe he was down the chimney delivering some trendy ankle boots. I stood there for ages, catching my breath, nose pressed up against the window, my mind blank.

'Gaby? What are you doing here?' Marisa appeared next to me. She looked very thin, dressed head to toe in black. Super trendy as always.

'I don't know,' I said, and that was the honest answer. 'I couldn't be at school any more.'

'Come inside, you must be freezing. Where's your coat?'

'I left it at school. It wasn't exactly an organized bunk off.' I stepped into the warmth of the shop, the hot air blasting me, setting my internal heating system all to cock. I now thought it was summer and started sweating.

'Let me get you a hot drink.'

'Can I have a drink of water instead please?'

She nodded and busied herself out the back getting water and also making me a hot chocolate from her frothy milk machine. There were quite a few people in the shop and she had Sally, her younger sister who didn't have kids, helping out. Sally waved from behind the till where a few people were waiting to pay.

'Come and sit down here and have your drink. Come on.' She patted the battered brown leather sofa at the back of the shop near the changing rooms. I sank down into the comfiness of it and gulped my water before slurping the scalding hot chocolate, burning my tongue in the process.

'We've missed you, Gaby,' Marisa said quietly, grabbing my free hand. 'I don't think I've seen you for months. Not since the funeral.' Ooooh, that felt like a conversational hand grenade. No one mentioned the funeral, like ever!

'Mmmm,' that was all she was going to get. I didn't trust myself to speak.

'Do you want to talk about it?'

'I don't know,' I said very quietly. Why had I come here?

'Your mum isn't here today; she's gone Christmas shopping.' I knew that. 'I can ring her if you like.' I shook my head.

'Have you had any lunch?' I shook my head again.

She stood up. 'Come on, you're coming with me.'

I levered myself out of the comforting, creaking sofa and stood up, leaving my empty drinks cups on the floor.

'I'm just popping home for a bit, Sally. You OK to hold the fort?'

'Aye, aye, cap'n!' And she saluted Marisa comedy-style.

We walked out of the shop and round the corner to Emily's road. Her house was right at the end, nearer my house than near the shops. I hadn't been to her house since she was alive. I felt quite sick, but somehow knew this was where I had to go . . .

'I have waffles in the freezer,' Marisa called out from the kitchen. I could hear her rooting around in the drawers, bags rustling and things being yanked this way and that. I was sitting in the living room, staring up at the black fireplace, just like our one at home, with framed pictures balanced precariously between the candlesticks and glass ornaments. Emily smiled out from two or three of them. Much younger and gap-toothed. There was one with me in it—the ice skating from last year. We have our arms round each other and look like we are about to topple over onto the ice. I think we did about a second later.

The Christmas tree was just as artfully decorated as our own, and on the fireplace there hung just one stocking instead of the usual two.

'Did you want some waffles? I've got maple syrup too, your favourite,' she asked, coming into the room.

'Does Emily ever come and visit you?' I asked out of the blue. Not quite the answer Marisa was looking for I think.

'What do you mean?' Marisa looked shocked.

'Like, does she come and hang out with you? Go shopping, watch TV, that sort of thing.'

Marisa went quiet. Then she said, 'Emily's dead, Gaby. You came to the funeral, remember?'

'I know she's dead. But do you still see her?'

'No. Do you?'

I wanted to say yes, but I had made a promise to Emily that I would never say. 'No, but I wish I did.' And then, like the floodgates had opened, a tidal wave of emotion overtook me and I burst into tears, howling great racking, snotty sobs, the sort that are just not attractive, no matter how gorgeous you are before you started. They wreck your face!

And before I knew it, I was buried in Marisa's bony chest. She was sobbing too, holding on to me like a life raft, each of us in our own private ocean of grief, bobbing along beside each other, reaching out for someone to make the pain go away. But it wouldn't go. No amount of pretending Emily was still here, that any minute she was going to walk in the door and start doing a stupid dance, could make up for the fact that inside me there was a gaping black hole that couldn't be filled. It was so unfair. 'Why did she have to die?' I cried out. 'I couldn't get to her; I didn't get there in time!' I lay in Marisa's arms crying, knowing I had to feel this, it had to be real, I had to know she was dead and that was it.

'Darling Gaby. I don't know why my beautiful girl had to die, but there was nothing you or anyone could have done to stop it. If I could have torn out my own heart to save her, I would have done.' Marisa was quietly crying. 'No one expects to bury their child. I miss her every day, I feel a half person, and every day I wish it wasn't so, but it is.' And just as she said that, a single white feather floated down from the ceiling and into the centre of the post-box-red rug.

'Will you look at that!' Marisa exclaimed. She wiped her eyes with the heels of her hands and stood up to collect the offering. 'Where did that come from?' She picked it up and studied it. 'It smells of chocolate.'

'It's from Emily,' I said, not caring if she believed or not or called for the men in white coats.

'I know.' She pressed it to her heart. 'I've a few more upstairs.'

'So have I,' I said, surprised but pleased it wasn't just Robbie and me that knew what they were.

'I get one when I'm having a really bad day. It will be in the drier, or on my car seat or inside my jumper. I had one in a loaf of bread one day, inside the plastic bag!'

'Wow! That's funny!' I giggled. The thought of finding a feather in a plastic bag. 'Can you imagine complaining to the shop manager saying your loaf of bread has been contaminated by an angel feather? They would be calling for the doctor to take you away.' We both collapsed into hysterical laughter, the kind that comes from nowhere when you have been at the other end of the scale moments before.

'I'll be back in a minute, stay there.' Marisa disappeared upstairs and came down with a pile of clothes and some photo albums.

'I've been meaning to bring these round, but somehow have never got the time.' She placed the pile on the floor. I picked up the first thing in the pile of clothes— it was Emily's purple Gap hoodie that she always wore at the weekends when we were slobbing. 'I want you to have her favourite clothes. She would want it too. I couldn't face giving them to charity and seeing someone else around town in them. It has to be you.' I leafed through the rest of the stuff, pretty dresses, skinny jeans, and a few mega-cool T-shirts that I had always loved on her. I put the hoodie on straight away. It smelt of her—all summery and fresh, Marisa's washing powder. I could feel a second wave of tears well up and I let them fall. Marisa stroked my arm. 'We'll get through this, Gaby. We have to, we have no choice.' I didn't know how she could be so strong. Emily was her daughter. And here was I having a nervous breakdown all over her. It should be *me* comforting *her.*

It was like she read my mind. 'Oh believe me, I have my moments. I'm having a good day today. Tomorrow, well, I'll deal with that tomorrow. Getting out of bed has been hard.'

I picked up the photo albums next and they were full of pictures of all of us: George, Millie, Rosie, and me. Robbie and Jake too—we all looked so young. I hadn't realized that Emily had done all this. Again, Marisa read my mind: 'Oh, Em didn't put all this together, Gus did. He needed a project, being a boy and not liking all the crying, so I asked him to make these albums. We have some too. They're fabulous, aren't they?' I agreed. And I got to keep one of them, which was even better.

'I'm going to ring the school now and your mum.' She disappeared off to find the phone and I sat there looking at the pictures. I really wanted to go upstairs though. So up I sneaked, listening for Marisa downstairs. I opened the door to Emily's room and the wind was knocked out of me. It was exactly the same. Her red spotty duvet was all smoothed out, her beads and bracelets hung on her hand-shaped jewellery holder on her dressing-table, next to a photo of her and me on our birthday a few years ago in the home-made jelly-bean frame I had created especially. Her bashed-up pink Converse were stuffed under the chair of the dressing-table and all her books and knick-knacks were still arranged just so on her shelves. It wasn't a dusty mausoleum at all, but like she had just popped out and was due back any second.

'It's just how she left it,' Marisa said behind me. 'One day we'll change it, but not yet. It's too soon. Do you want to take anything?'

I looked around, and something caught my eye on the jewellery holder. It was the gold heart-shaped pendant we had given each other for our birthdays a few months ago, with our names and Friends Forever engraved on either side. I always wore the identical one round my neck when I wasn't at school 'This please.' Marisa nodded and I hooked it round my neck so she could do it up for me.

'Your mum's on her way. Don't be a stranger, hey. We love seeing you. Any time.' And we had a big big hug right there in Emily's room. I knew right then for sure Emily was never coming back, that she had sent me to her mum and that I would be round to visit everyone here any time I liked. It didn't make any of it OK, not one bit, but it made it real.

feathers Anonymous unite!

The bus to school was always going to be embarrassing. And somewhat scary after my excursion down nutjob street yesterday. I was on my own now, no more Emily holding my hand. I was Gaby Richards, facing the world, being in it, as Emily said I had to. I got to the bus stop before anyone else. Standing there in the cold, stamping my feet, I wondered what being in the world really meant. Was I going to discover a cure for cancer? Just being happy would be a start.

'Hey,' a voice said behind me. It was Francesca.

'What are you doing at this stop? I thought you got on the next one down.'

'I thought I would try and get a better seat on the bus today,' she smiled.

'Where do you live?' I asked.

'Bancroft Road.' That was actually nearer this bus stop than the one she got on.

'What happened to you yesterday?' she asked kindly and not at all in a gossipy manner.

'Oh, that. Hmm.' I had no idea what to say.

'You don't have to talk about it.'

'I'm sort of dreading going in after how I acted in the canteen. It wasn't the best move.'

'Was it because they didn't have lamb hotpot? That's enough to drive anyone over the edge.' She smiled cheekily at me and made me laugh.

'Something like that.'

Rosie, George, and Millie turned up and I surprised myself by feeling vaguely disappointed. It was nice just talking to Francesca.

'Yabba, you got over the bug? Did you run off and vom?' Rosie asked. Of course, no one knew what happened. I had just run off. I could say anything. My phone and stuff was all still at school. I was wearing my parka today—not uniform, but allowed in the circumstances.

'I was worried that I might have it, so got sent home.'

'Good move,' George said. 'You missed Mr Blank and one of his surprise tests!'

Result!

I was the first on the bus for the way home. I don't know where the others were. Someone plonked down next to me. Francesca. She looked nervous. 'Look, I'm just going to say this, OK? Tell me to shut up at any point. Did you freak out yesterday because of Emily?' I nodded. 'I found another white feather after you left, like the one that fell from the ceiling. They're from her, aren't they?' I nodded. Where was this going? 'I think she's trying to tell you she's still here looking out for you and wants you to be happy.' I nodded again.

'I know this because I've had them too.'

'What, from Emily?' I almost shouted.

'No! I don't know who from, but maybe my grandad, my mum's dad. I was very close to him. They are messages to help you when you're feeling rubbish.'

'How do you know all this?' I asked, astounded there was yet another member of Feathers Anonymous. It was catching!

'I told you, my mum is into it all. She loves the whole angel feather thing. I didn't believe her at first, but then

I started getting them too, just like she was. When Dad disappeared, we were left with no house—it had to be sold as part of the divorce. And because Dad had to pay for it all, he and Mum couldn't send me to my old school any more, so I had to come here. We had to have a smaller house, while Dad moved in with the woman he left us for and her daughter, who goes to the posh school that I'd just left. She used to be my best friend.' My jaw dropped. How hideous!

'Are you still friends?' I asked, horrified.

'No, I don't see anyone from there any more. It was so so awful. I had to cut off from it all. It was too . . . embarrassing, like something from a really bad soap. Mum practically had a nervous breakdown most days. It has got a lot better, but she still cries a lot. I see Dad in the week and every other weekend. I never want to go to his new house, ever! He comes to ours and Mum goes out. Or we go out for dinner. I hate it, I wish he'd never left and I miss him, so does Mum.' Her face clouded over for a second and I could see all the pain that was hiding in there. 'Anyway when it all kicked off, we kept getting the feathers. Inside clothes or once inside a packet of frozen peas!' It was like someone had cut the edit button in Francesca's normally reserved manner, and her mouth was running away with her! It was quite spectacularly mad. I felt sane for once.

'No way!' And I told her about Marisa and the loaf of bread. 'Do you still get the feathers?'

'We do, sometimes, but at the moment, not so much. Mum has got a job and loves it so that's good. But she is just so sad. It's like Dad died.' She and Marisa should hang out together! 'Hey, do you think anyone else gets the feathers from Emily?' Francesca asked eagerly. 'What about Robbie? He saw the one you got yesterday. He ran after you.'

'He did?' I pretended I'd never seen him.

'Yes, but you must have run like the wind because he came back and left with Jake.' She lapsed into silence as the bus gradually filled up. The girls got on and sat behind us, said hi and everything. Robbie and Jake got on. Just seeing Jake made my stomach flip, not with dread, but with excitement. He liked me. Although perhaps not any more though, not after the way I had been acting.

Somewhere in my head a little voice just urged me to wave. It was my voice, but I wondered if Emily was subtly pushing me. Jake looked over as he stuffed his bag in the parcel shelf above his seat. I smiled at him and waved. He just stared and then looked behind him to see who I was waving at. He did a mock, 'Who, me?' jokey mime and I nodded and laughed. He gave me the most happy smile and waved back, his ears burning, and turned round and sat down. I wondered what would happen now . . .

'Yabba, did I see you just *wave* to Jake?' George observed.

'What have I missed?' Millie gasped. 'What what what?'

'Yabba waved at Jake,' Rosie filled her in. 'Why did you do that? You ditched him at the weekend.'

'Hmmm, he looked cute?' I said smiling through my casual answer, heart beating in my ears.

'Gaby! You sly thing!' George marvelled. 'Have you been watching that new dating show for hot tips? Treat him mean, keep him keen?'

I shook my head while the girls set up watch to see what Jake would do next.

'So what you doing this weekend?' Francesca asked shyly after a moment. The bus had started up.

'Oh, I don't know.'

'Do you want to do something?' She looked at me, as if expecting laughing, or me to say no or to start running a mile like all the other times.

'Er . . .' I didn't know what to say. Right now, getting through the day was an achievement. Having to make a decision on my own was way out of my comfort zone!

'You don't have to. It's just a thought.' She smiled hopefully at me.

'What did you have in mind?' I felt like I was considering a date.

'I've got that new comedy on DVD; we could watch that at mine.'

What was the alternative? Sitting in my room? Talking to myself for real this time?

'OK, that would be great,' I said rather hesitantly, unsure I had made the right decision, but at least I had made it on my own.

Before she could say anything Alex butted in. 'Oooh, get you two, getting all excited over some DVD. Nice work, ladies. I guess you two piggies in the middle don't get out much.' It was Alexandra Bennett earwigging our conversation and smiling sympathetically, like we needed special help with our social skills or something.

'Why don't you go and help your mum in her charity shop, darling. I'm sure she needs Britain's Next Top Model to help with the shelf stacking!' Where had that come from? Did *I* say it? That would have hurt because we all knew her mum ran the rival shop to The Brown Bag.

The girls looked up from their conversation, slack jawed. Francesca winced, waiting for the returning insult.

I just brazened it out, jaw firm, astonished that I had even attempted to retaliate.

Alex looked stunned, like I had electrocuted her. No one ever gave her a telling off. One of the Kool Aids giggled, but was silenced with a haughty glare. She raised an eyebrow at me, sucked in her cheeks and turned round, ears aflame!

Francesca put her hand up for a high five and it took all my inner calm not to burst out laughing.

'Way to go, Yabba,' George whispered. 'Welcome back to the land of the living.'

'Thanks,' I said and winked at Francesca, making her giggle. 'Can I just ask you something, Francesca?'

'Yes?'

'What's your favourite chocolate?'

'That's easy. Dime bars! Why?'

'No reason, just checking,' and I smiled to myself. At that moment, I knew for certain I had made the right decision.

EPILOGUE
SEPTEMBER

'Thank you for coming,' Marisa said quietly. 'It means a lot to Dave, Gus, and me.'

We all stood in their back garden, the brilliant September sunshine dappling the lawn through the trees with golden light, the yellow-tipped leaves flickering up and down in the gentle breeze. 'A special thank you to Gaby who gave up her big birthday party.' I smiled. How could I do anything else? Emily had been my best friend. And I fiddled with the chain around my neck with both gold heart pendants looped through, jangling together.

Marisa was holding a bunch of white helium balloons. 'Today would have been Emily's fourteenth birthday and we felt we needed to mark the day as it was so close to the day that she died.' I looked around at the people gathered there. Me, George, Rosie, Millie, Robbie, Jake, Gus, Max, Mum, Dad, Emily's grandparents, her Aunt Sally, Aunt Vicky and Uncle Pete and her cousins. There was a balloon for each of us. The adults were sipping champagne. Marisa was determined this would be a celebration and not a tragic tear-stained affair. 'The balloons have a tag attached to each of them with enough space to write a birthday message if you feel you want to.' That had been my idea! I knew Emily would have liked that. Marisa handed out the balloons to all of us with coloured pencils to write our message.

I took mine and leant against a tree. 'What are you going to write?' Jake asked. 'I can't think of anything.'

I stared at him with his furrowed brow trying to be all thoughtful and emotional and my stomach flipped, like it always did when I looked at him.

'Oh Jake, why not be original and say Happy Birthday?' I teased him.

He pinched my arm, not unkindly, and smiled his stomach-churning, faint-inducing smile that got me every time. How had it taken me so long to decide whether he could be my boyfriend? It all seemed so easy now that he was. I should have listened to Emily all along—she is, was, always right. I wondered if she was watching and doing the 'I told you so' dance . . .

He put his arm protectively around his card like he was doing a test and didn't want me to copy and made a big song and dance about what he was writing.

I looked at my card. It wasn't big enough to tell Emily everything that had happened in the last year. I am sure she knew anyway. I still got the occasional feather when I woke in a panic that I hadn't saved her from the accident or for some reason was plunged into a cave of darkness that didn't have a speck of light. But on those days I could also turn to my friends for support. I had learnt to trust other people, and believe that not everyone was going to do a runner or die and leave me alone, not yet, anyway.

I wrote:

Still BFFs, no matter what. I miss you,
but I am being in the world like you wanted
me to be, and it's OK.
Love always, Gaby xxx

When everyone was ready, we gathered together and collectively let the balloons go, carried away on the warm breeze, their messages sent heavenwards. I knew Emily was OK, that she wasn't lonely or sad because she had told me everything was cool where she was. And I always believed what she said. She had probably been promoted now to a higher level of angel, anyway. And that made me smile, her bossing some newbies about.

'Guys, we better go,' Robbie said about an hour later in the early evening. 'She'll be wondering where we are.'

'Where are we going?' I asked again for the millionth time.

'It's a surprise!' George said. 'Be patient!'

We said goodbyes to everyone; I hugged Marisa, knowing I would be popping in for tea next Wednesday, our weekly treat. I looked forward to it. She would get me stuff from the shop that she couldn't sell at the end of the season and I was so well dressed now!

'Have a great time, love!' Mum called out. 'We'll see you later.'

Jake took my hand and we followed the others down the street and headed in the direction of the park. It was a totally beautiful evening, and we were still in our summer clothes, there wasn't even a hint of autumnal breeze in the air that you sometimes get this time of year, beckoning the end of long days and welcoming winter into the fold. The park reflected this too with bright-green leaves and only a hint of orange to be seen.

'The picnic area she said,' Robbie called back as he hiked up the grass to the gated dog-free area under the trees. I could see some purple balloons tethered to one of the picnic benches and a piñata tied up to one of the trees! 'Where is she?' As we got closer I spotted that the picnic table was all decked out with a purple tablecloth, paper cups and plates, and lots of cakes and nibbles.

'Wow!' I said. 'I really wasn't expecting this.'

'Hey, I'm over here!' and down jumped Francesca from the tree next to the opposite picnic bench. 'Look what I found!'

'What are you doing climbing trees?' Robbie asked, all concerned. 'We weren't here in case you had an accident.'

'Chill, Rob, I'm OK. Quite capable of looking after myself.'

'So what did you find?' Millie asked.

Robbie stood protectively next to Francesca, taking her hand in his and playing with her silver ring on her little finger, looking like he had won the lotto.

'This.' And she unfurled her hand to reveal a burst white balloon with a tag attached to it. 'I saw it drift into the tree while I was waiting for you guys to turn up. How was it, by the way?'

'Yeah, it was lovely,' Rosie said. 'Not sad, but sad if you know what I mean.' Francesca nodded.

'This is too weird,' George whispered. 'We only just let those balloons go an hour or so ago. I thought it would have gone for miles.'

'Which one is it?' I asked, knowing that I didn't even need to ask at all. It would be mine.

It was. 'Have it,' Francesca said to me.

'No, I have a feeling it's for you,' I said, pushing her hand back to her.

Francesca smiled at me. 'Happy birthday, you.' And she hugged me hard, knowing this was my first ever birthday on my own without Emily.

But the great thing was, I wasn't on my own, was I?

Photo © name of photographer

AbOUt tHE AUtHOR

Janet has worked as a book-seller children's book editor, and DJ with her best friend (under the name 'Britney and Whitney'). She spent her childhood making comics and filling notebooks with stories. In fact, her old boss at Bloomsbury thought she had such a talent for writing, he asked her to write a joke book, which she did with her brother.

Janet lives in London and draws constant inspiration from her three, brilliant children. *Gaby's Angel* is her first book for Oxford University Press.

More
Oxford books
you might
enjoy . . .

THE GRIMM LEGACY
Polly Shulman

Borrow the

magic ...

if you dare!

ISBN: 978-019-279310-2

CLUBBING TOGETHER
Helena Pielichaty

—++—o—++—

Meet the fabulous,

fun,

feisty

girls,

Sammie, Brody, Alex,

and Jolene!

—++—o—++—

ISBN: 978-0-19-275430-1

FROZEN IN TIME
Ali Sparkes

Get ready

for a

heart-stopping

adventure!

ISBN: 978-0-19-273400-6